"I Can't Den[...] Must Deny Us Bo[...]"

Lydia said. "We can't act on these feelings. It w[...] be wrong."

"It would be wrong if we don't. Can't you see that?" Wade asked. He searched Lydia's eyes for the answer he wanted. Desire as hot and consuming as what he felt shone in their golden depths, but restraint held that longing in check. "It's not going to stop until we have each other."

"This has to be goodbye," Lydia said. "Otherwise, we're going to destroy each other."

He wanted to argue with her, but he knew his words would be useless. She was a lady, and there was no way he could force her to forget her moral upbringing, her regard for propriety and her personal sense of right and wrong. Those were all qualities he admired. But right now, he wished she were a little bit more woman and a little less lady....

Dear Reader,

Annette Broadrick fans (and you know who you all are!) rejoice. Annette's *Man of the Month, Where There Is Love,* is here! This is the story you've all been waiting for: superspy Max Moran *finally* meets his match! I'm not going to tell you a single thing about this fantastic book; you've just got to read it for yourselves.

May is also chock-full of books by authors I know you love. Let's start with BJ James's *Tears of the Rose,* written in BJ's uniquely unforgettable style. Next, Leslie Davis Guccione returns with *Rough and Ready,* a title that describes her hero perfectly!

Expect the unexpected in Joan Johnston's *A Little Time in Texas,* and thrill to Justine Davis's dramatic *Upon the Storm.* And last, but not least, is *Talk of the Town* by Beverly Barton, in which it's not just the weather that gets steamy in Riverton, Mississippi.

As for next month . . . well, you're all in for an exciting treat. Believe it or not, it's the ten-year anniversary of Silhouette Desire, which was launched back in June 1982. To celebrate, I've convinced six of your favorite Desire authors to participate in a very special program, JUNE GROOMS, in which six sinfully sexy heroes are saying goodbye to the single life—forever. Don't miss it!

All the best,

Lucia Macro
Senior Editor

BEVERLY BARTON

TALK OF THE TOWN

SILHOUETTE *Desire*®

Published by Silhouette Books New York

America's Publisher of Contemporary Romance

SILHOUETTE BOOKS
300 East 42nd St., New York, N.Y. 10017

TALK OF THE TOWN

ISBN: 0-373-05711-3

First Silhouette Books printing May 1992

Printed in the U.S.A.

Books by Beverly Barton

Silhouette Desire

Yankee Lover #580
Lucky in Love #628
Out of Danger #662
Sugar Hill #687
Talk of the Town #711

BEVERLY BARTON

has been in love with romance since her grandfather gave her an illustrated book of *Beauty and the Beast*. An avid reader since childhood, she began writing at the age of nine, and wrote short stories, poetry, plays and novels throughout high school and college. After marriage to her own ''hero'' and the births of her daughter and son, she chose to be a full-time home-maker, a.k.a. wife, mother, friend and volunteer.

Six years ago, she began substitute teaching and re-turned to writing as a hobby. In 1987, she joined the Romance Writers of America and soon afterward helped found the Heart of Dixie chapter in Alabama. Her hobby became an obsession as she devoted more and more time to improving her skills as a writer. Now, her lifelong dream of being published has come true.

To my dear friend and an avid romance reader
Helen Everett,
to whom my family and I owe an eternal debt of gratitude;

and special thanks to my daughter
Badiema,
who believed in me even when I didn't believe in myself

Prologue

Wade Cameron hurled into the hospital emergency room, his brown leather jacket dotted with raindrops and his wavy black hair plastered to his head. Quickly scanning the room for a familiar face, he recognized the guard walking toward him.

"Hell of a night," Lester Cummings said. "Sorry about what happened to Macie." He removed his uniform cap and scratched his bald head. "More wrecks on a night like this than any other time."

"Where is she, Les?" Wade asked.

"They whisked her and Mayor Reid, both, on up to surgery," Lester said, shaking his head. "Damn shame."

"Where's surgery?" Wade wanted to take the older man by the shoulders and shake him soundly. He didn't have time for this idle chitchat. His wife could be dying. And though the term was laughable when it came to Macie, she was still his wife, legally at least, even if emotionally she'd ceased being anything but a nuisance years ago.

"Second floor. Take a right just through those doors. The elevator goes straight up to the surgery waiting room."

Wade rushed past Lester and all the curious stares coming from the other people in the emergency room. When the sheriff's deputy had come by the farm to tell Wade about the car wreck, he had advised him to hurry.

"Mrs. Reid's up there," Lester said just as Wade left the room.

The elevator doors stood open as if waiting for him. Wade stepped inside, pushed Two and leaned back against the wall. Mrs. Reid? The mayor's wife? he wondered. It was reasonable to assume, since she lived in town, she would have gotten here quicker than he did. Even though he'd driven as fast as his old truck would go, it had still taken him fifteen minutes to drive in from the farm.

He was racking his brain trying to remember the mayor's wife, when the elevator doors opened and he saw her pacing up and down the hallway outside the waiting room. Yeah, he remembered her, all right. Four years ago when Tyler Reid had run for mayor, he'd used his beautiful bride to full advantage. Wade doubted there was a person in all of Riverton, in all of northeast Mississippi for that matter, who hadn't been introduced to the former Alabama debutante.

The sound of the elevator doors closing behind him prompted Wade to move. He guessed he should say something to Mrs. Reid, but what the hell did a guy say in a situation like this? Sorry your husband and my wife were in a bad wreck tonight, but if they hadn't been carrying on an illicit affair, none of this would have happened.

Just as he moved in her direction, she stopped pacing and turned toward him. Wade felt a huge emptiness in the pit of his stomach when he looked at her tear-stained, mesmerizing, hazel-green eyes. He'd only seen her a couple of times over the years, mostly at a distance, and he'd forgotten how incredibly lovely she was. Her lips parted as if she was about to speak to him, and then some man with carrot-red hair came up beside her and placed his arm around her shoulders.

Wade had an irrational desire to go over and jerk the man away from her and tell him that if she needed comfort, he'd give it. Wade shook his head, then walked past the couple and into the waiting room.

Well, what the hell was he supposed to do now? he wondered. Just sit and wait for... for what? Shouldn't there be a nurse on duty to tell people what was going on? Maybe he should find somebody—a doctor, a nurse, even a damned orderly—anybody who could tell him what was happening with Macie.

"Do you have someone in surgery?" Lydia Reid asked.

Wade looked at her. She had stepped inside the waiting room, her valiant protector at her side. "Yeah, my wife."

"Oh. Are you Mr. Cameron?" Her spine stiffened and the casually friendly look on her face softened to one of pity.

"Yeah, Wade Cameron." He offered his hand.

She simply stared, noticing that his hand was large and brown, and his big, blunt fingers were sprinkled with black hair. Obviously a strong man, Lydia thought, but she couldn't help wondering if he felt as weak and helpless as she did right now.

The red-haired man reached around Lydia Reid and took Wade's hand. "I'm Glenn Haraway, a friend of the family." After the handshake, Glenn escorted her to a nearby couch. "This has been a ghastly night for Lydia. I'm afraid it's all been a bit much for her."

Wade surveyed young Mr. Haraway and forced himself to suppress a smile. Immaculately dressed in an expensive suit, his hair perfectly styled, and an "educated" Southern accent dripping from his lips, this friend of the family obviously wanted to be much more to Mrs. Reid. But it was just as obvious that Mrs. Reid didn't have the foggiest notion she was the object of the man's desire.

"They told me downstairs that Macie and Reid are both in surgery." Wade spoke to Haraway, but he watched Lydia.

Her eyes met his, sunshine-fresh hazel and midnight black colliding in a battle of questions and accusations and silent pleas. "I'm afraid they couldn't wait to get your signature on the release papers, Mr. Cameron," Lydia said. "I understand immediate surgery was required or your wife would have died."

"Yeah, Deputy Grissom said it was bad." Wade hadn't missed the mixture of resentment and sympathy in her voice, and he wondered if she blamed herself for her husband's infidelity and perhaps him for Macie's.

"The nurse wanted to be notified as soon as you arrived so you could sign those papers," Haraway said. "The nurses' station is down the hall."

"Thanks." Immediately Wade left the room.

"Seems like a nice enough fellow," Glenn said as he sat down beside Lydia.

"But not nice enough to hold his wife's interest." Lydia bit down on her lower lip in an effort to ward off the tears choking her. This simply couldn't be happening. Tyler was near death and all she could think about was the fact that he'd been having an affair with Macie Cameron, the best-known whore in the whole county.

"You don't know for sure—" Glenn said.

"Yes, I do."

"Mother should have kept her mouth shut. Why she thought it necessary to fill you in on all the details when we were trying to leave for the hospital, I'll never know." Glenn patted Lydia on the back and reached to take her trembling hand into his steady grasp.

"Someone should have told me months ago." Lydia jerked her hand away and stood up. "No, years ago."

When Glenn followed her across the room and tried to comfort her, she turned on him. "You knew, didn't you? Of course you knew. You're his best friend . . . his business associate. How long?'' She grabbed the lapels of Glenn Haraway's coat and glared directly into his startled blue eyes. ''How long has Tyler been unfaithful to me, and... with... with how many women?''

''Please, don't ask me such a question.'' Glenn dropped his head, apparently unable to look her in the eye.

''I know Macie Cameron wasn't the first. Your mother as good as said so tonight.''

''Damn Mother! She had no right to start rattling like that.'' Glenn placed his neatly manicured fingers at his throat and began fiddling with his silk tie, loosening the perfect knot. ''Tyler loves you. He's always loved you, but he's not like most of us. He can't be satisfied with... with just one woman.''

''Oh.'' It shouldn't hurt so much, she thought, but it did. Of course, it really hadn't come as a surprise. She'd known for quite some time that things weren't right in her marriage, but she had purposely chosen to ignore all the warning signs. For over two years now she had been pretending, with herself and with Tyler, because she hadn't had the courage to face the truth. Even when Tyler had stopped coming to her for sex nearly a year ago, she'd convinced herself that desire ended in most marriages after a while.

''Don't think it was you, Lydia.'' Glenn reached out for her again, and again she withdrew from him. ''You're the most wonderful woman, a perfect wife. Any man would be proud to call you his own.''

''Any man except my husband.''

''Tyler is extremely proud of you.''

She laughed, a tight, dry laugh filled with all the rage brewing inside her. ''I wanted a child. Did Tyler ever tell you that? He kept saying someday.''

''Tyler will make a great father one of these days, you wait and see.'' Glenn rubbed his hands together, massaging the knuckles with the tips of his fingers. ''You have to understand that these other women don't mean anything.''

She jerked her head around and glared at him, her eyes wide open and overly bright. "Obviously I don't either."

"Lydia, you must understand that there are...well, some men like certain things...things they would never expect their wives to..."

Her loud, deep-throated laughter filled the waiting room, destroying the morbid silence. Glenn looked at her, a shocked expression on his face.

"My God, Lydia, what's wrong with you?"

When he tried to grab her, she swatted his hands away. "Leave me alone. I'm all right." Her laughter died as quickly as it had been born.

"Please sit down and try to stay calm," Glenn suggested. "I'll go downstairs and get us some coffee."

"Yes, thank you, please do." Right now, she realized, she would have agreed to almost anything to be rid of Glenn and his inadequate defense of Tyler's unforgivable actions.

Wade Cameron watched the other man enter the elevator before he returned to the waiting room. He hadn't planned on going back, but when he'd passed by and heard Lydia Reid arguing with ol' friend-of-the-family, he'd stopped and listened. Her near hysterical laughter had chilled him to the bone. He knew exactly what she was feeling—all the pain and anger threatening to explode inside her, and he understood what it felt like to think yourself unloved and inadequate. But his pain and anger were old wounds, long since healed. His love for Macie had died a few months after their wedding when he discovered she'd lied to him about being pregnant, and what little was left of their marriage had ended less than a year later, when he found her in the barn with one of the hired hands.

And now, seven years after making Macie Whitten his bride, he was free once again. He'd wanted Macie out of his life, but he'd never wanted her dead.

When he'd found the nurses' station and told them who he was, they'd handed him the permission papers to sign.

Less than two minutes later the doctor had appeared, informing him that Macie had died on the operating table.

He couldn't understand why it hurt so. He hadn't loved her. For years she'd made his life a living hell. He should feel a sense of relief that all the misery was over, instead of anger and frustration and sorrow. Macie had been bad, but not evil, selfish but not cruel. And she'd been a very unhappy woman who sought to ease her misery with sex.

Wade wondered how he was going to tell his daughter Molly that her mother was dead. Even though Macie hadn't been much of a mother, Molly had loved her, had tried in every way possible to gain her mother's love and attention. His child didn't deserve this. She had already endured far too much in her brief six years of life.

He stood just inside the waiting room and watched Lydia Reid as she wrapped her arms across her chest and squeezed her upper arms tightly. She seemed to be looking out the windows at the rock garden below, and he wondered if he should say something to her, try to comfort her in some way, before he left.

As if sensing his presence, she turned around slowly. Her face was serene, her eyes dry. He could tell she'd taken control of her emotions. She was a strong woman even if she did look soft and fragile. He tried to speak, but couldn't. It was as if she were asking him not to talk, her bright hazel eyes pleading for a few more moments of silence.

God, she was beautiful! Delicately built, her slender body blossomed into ripe curves above and below her tiny waist. Her gold-streaked brown hair hung to her shoulders, the ends curling from the dampness outside. Why on earth Tyler Reid had ever been unfaithful to this woman, he'd never understand.

"Are you all right?" Wade asked, wanting to take her in his arms. The very idea was crazy, but he couldn't dismiss the notion that she needed his comfort.

"You found the nurses' station?" She looked away from him, finding it impossible to keep staring into those dark,

dark eyes. She couldn't bear seeing the pain that paralleled her own.

"Yeah."

"We haven't heard anything, yet." She began pacing around the room, nervously eyeing the clock, scanning the hallway for movement, anything to escape Wade Cameron's intense gaze. "Glenn has gone downstairs for coffee."

Why didn't he say something else? she wondered. He was just standing there in the doorway watching her. She couldn't understand why he made her feel so uncomfortable when it was obvious he felt sorry for her. Glenn had tried to comfort her in the worst way possible—by making excuses for Tyler's infidelity. Soon the whole town would know about Tyler and Macie Cameron, if they didn't already. And everyone would know that she knew. The thought of all those pitying stares, all those whispered innuendos, filled Lydia's veins with icy fear.

Did Wade Cameron pity her? Was that why he was looking at her so oddly? Well, he needn't waste his sympathy on her when, after all, he was in the same predicament as she. Or was he?

"Please stop looking at me that way." She tried to meet his unflinching stare.

"What way?" Didn't she realize that he knew what she was going through, that he understood, only too well?

"I don't need your pity. Save it for yourself."

"I quit feeling sorry for myself a long time ago. I made a big mistake marrying Macie, but I've paid dearly for it. I'd say you're still paying for your mistake."

"My mistake?" How dare he insinuate that her marriage to Tyler had been a mistake. It had been a fairy-tale courtship and wedding, a union of two old Southern families.

"Your marriage is none of my business, but I think—"

"You're quite correct, Mr. Cameron, my marriage is none of your business."

"Sorry." He turned to leave just as a doctor dressed in green scrubs walked up behind him.

"Lydia." The doctor walked past Wade and took Lydia Reid's hands.

"Oh, Bick, how is he?" she asked. "Is he going to be all right?"

"Lydia, my dear—"

"No, no..."

"We did everything we could, but it wasn't enough. I'm so sorry."

From all the way across the room, Wade could feel her pain. He wanted to go to her, take her in his arms and tell her that everything would be all right. He didn't. He couldn't. He had no right to touch her. He was a stranger, a stranger who was mourning his own wife's death. But his own grief didn't stop him from desperately wanting to comfort another man's widow.

One

It's him! she thought, taking another quick look at the big, dark man in the faded jeans and tan Stetson. What was he doing here? Lydia Reid slipped behind a row of Boston ferns hanging from the ceiling inside Clement's Feed and Seed Store. Her heart raced wildly as she sought a hiding place.

During the two months since Tyler's death, no one had mentioned the name Cameron to her. Not once. For days after her husband's death, she hadn't been allowed more than a few minutes alone during the day, and at night her mother, sister-in-law or brother seemed to have taken turns checking on her. But they had carefully sidestepped any mention of the peculiar circumstances surrounding Tyler Reid's tragic demise.

Of course, Glenn and Eloise had practically moved in. And the entire town had been parading in and out, bringing food and flowers and showering her with sympathy. Everyone had deliberately avoided any mention of Macie Cameron or the fact that she had been killed in the same crash that had taken Mayor Reid's life. It was as if the townspeople as a whole had decided to try to protect her from the ugly truth.

During the weeks since that horrible night when she'd first met Wade Cameron, she had found herself thinking of him often. Too often. Luckily they didn't travel in the same social circles so it had been easy to avoid him. But unless she found some way to slip away unnoticed, she was going to have to face him today.

Lydia bent her head slightly to peep beneath the ferns. Wade Cameron was talking to another man, a man as big and dark as he. Although the other man wore a beard, and ugly scars marred the left side of his forehead and neck, it was obvious the two were brothers. The resemblance was unmistakable.

"When I finish up here, I'm going over to Lewey's for a beer," Wade said.

"Tanya and I'll meet your over there," the other man said. "She's up at Billings looking for a new Sunday dress."

When Wade's brother turned to go, Wade put his hand on the younger man's shoulder. "Britt?"

"Hey, I'm all right. You've got your own problems, don't worry about me."

Lydia felt like an eavesdropper, hiding there listening to a private conversation. Obviously the younger Cameron brother had some personal problems that were worrying Wade.

Lydia turned around. On each side of her were two long aisles of summer flowers ready for planting. Behind her was the back wall, covered with stacks of lawn fertilizer. If she had known Wade Cameron would be at Clement's Feed and Seed today, she would have waited until Monday to pick up the newly arrived rose bush she'd ordered.

Lost in her thoughts of how she could escape, Lydia didn't hear his approach.

"Hello," Wade Cameron said.

Lydia jumped at the unexpected sound of his voice. Trying valiantly to control her trembling hands, she slowly turned to face him.

"Hello, Mr. Cameron."

A quivering sensation spread through her stomach, and suddenly she felt light-headed. He looked the way she'd remembered him from the hospital, and she *had* remembered him, more often than she'd wanted to in the past two months. There was something so utterly masculine about the man, an aura of strength that drew Lydia to him.

"Never thought I'd see you in the Feed and Seed Store." He watched her while he spoke. Her pink cheeks and overbright eyes indicated embarrassment, and he hated that she felt so uneasy around him.

"Why's that?" Mercy, she hadn't realized he was so tall. He had to be at least a couple of inches over six feet.

"I just figured you had a gardener that took care of all the dirty work."

His eyes were even darker than she remembered, so brown they looked as black as his hair.

"We do...that is, I do have a gardener, but he doesn't touch my roses." Lydia took a deep breath trying to steady her nerves. Overpowering the earthy smell of rich earth and flowering plants, Wade Cameron's masculine aroma and the hint of a clean, citrus after-shave swamped Lydia's senses. "I...came by today to pick up my new rose bush. Clyde ordered me a new Tropicana."

"Tropicana?" He'd forgotten just how delicate Lydia Reid looked, all pale skin and small bones.

"It's a red-orange rose." She wished he would stop talking to her and go away. His very nearness disturbed her more than she wanted to admit.

"You and my mother would get along just fine." Wade laughed, thinking what an unlikely pair Lydia Reid and his mother would make. The fair fragile rose and a tough hardy weed.

"Oh?"

"She's got a green thumb. Can make anything grow."

They stood there, staring at each other. Several patrons of the feed and seed store gave Lydia and Wade some curious glances as they walked around them. From the other side of the ferns, Lydia heard female voices.

"It's that Cameron man," a plump gray-haired matron whispered. "He's talking to Lydia. Oh, my. Oh, my."

"Whatever could those two have to say to each other?" the other woman asked.

"Discussing that horrible night, no doubt."

"Shh... You wouldn't want them to overhear you."

Lydia knew her face had turned red. If only a hole would appear in the dirt floor beneath her feet, she would gladly crawl inside and pull the hole in after her.

"I was fixing to head over to Lewey's for a beer," Wade said, hoping to distract Lydia's attention from the two busybodies one aisle over. "Why don't you come with me and get some tea."

Go with him? Yes. That's exactly what she wanted to do. It didn't make any sense, but somehow she felt as if he alone understood the nightmare she'd been living through the past two months. On some level she was afraid of Wade Cameron and the unforgivable attraction she felt for him, but on a deeper, more primitive level, she longed for his care and protection.

"I...I don't know... if I should," she stammered, torn between two basic desires—the desire to maintain her reputation and the desire to be with Wade Cameron.

"Come on." He reached out, but stopped just short of touching her. "It's a hot day and it's getting crowded in here."

"I suppose it would be all right."

"You want to pick up your rose bush first or come back for it?"

"I think I'll get it later."

When he started to place his hand on her arm in a maneuvering gesture, she stepped around him and walked

down the aisle, then turned into the next one. Following her,
Wade tipped his hat and nodded to the two busybodies who
stood, with mouths agape, watching Lydia and Wade walk
past them.

"Good day, ladies," he said.

"How are you today, Lydia?" one woman asked.

"Fine, thank you." Lydia hastened her step, longing to be
free from prying eyes and wagging tongues.

"Beautiful weather we're having," the other matron said,
a catty smile on her face.

Wade placed his hand in the small of Lydia's back. He felt
her stiffen and then relax, slowing her steps. Together they
walked outside onto the sidewalk in front of the feed and
seed store. Like transparent gold, bright June sunshine
spread over the sleepy little Mississippi town. Since not even
a wisp of a breeze stirred, the ninety-degree temperature
seemed even warmer.

While they walked up the block toward Lewey's, neither
Wade nor Lydia spoke. Both were vividly aware of his big
hand resting protectively on the small of her back. She knew
she should move away; he knew he should drop his hand.

Townspeople on the streets and inside the shops watched
in fascination as Mayor Reid's widow and Macie Cameron's former husband entered the local diner. Lydia could
feel the curious stares, but refused to acknowledge anyone.

Lewey's wasn't much more than a hole-in-the-wall, con-
sisting of an L-shaped bar with round, swivel stools and five
booths, two facing the huge outside window. Instinctively
Wade led Lydia to a side booth, wanting to give them privacy and protect her from being on public display by the
window.

Easing into the booth, she kept her eyes downcast. Wade
removed his Stetson and hung it on the nearby hat rack before slipping into the booth on the opposite side.

Instantly a teenage boy appeared, a pad and pencil in his
hands. "Yeah, Wade, what'll it be for you and the lady?"

"Tea?" Wade asked, noticing the way Lydia was looking down at her hands, which she'd placed in her lap.

She raised her head and looked at him, a faint smile crossing her face. "Unsweetened tea with lemon, please."

"One iced tea and one beer," Wade told the boy who scribbled the order down and whirled away.

An antique jukebox in the corner of the diner caught Lydia's attention when an old Eddy Arnold tune began to play. Although she'd lived in Riverton for over four years, she'd never been in Lewey's. Glancing around, she realized why. Obviously this place was a blue-collar hangout.

"How have you been, really?" Wade's voice was low and deep, his gaze fixed directly on the woman sitting across from him—the woman whose very presence here with him seemed like a dream.

"It hasn't been easy." *That's an understatement,* she thought. "Everyone has been so overprotective. It's as if they think the truth can't hurt me if no one mentions it."

"That's made it worse, hasn't it?"

"Yes." He seemed to be the only person who understood, really understood. Nothing could protect her from reality. Her husband was dead. He had been fatally injured in an automobile wreck along with his latest lover. Tyler Dodson Reid, Riverton, Mississippi's golden boy, had gone to meet his Maker at the tender age of thirty-one. And he had left behind a wife who was not only confused and uncertain about the present and the future, but was eaten alive by feelings of inadequacy and failure.

"Would you believe me if I told you that, in time, all the gossip, all the stares and pitying looks won't bother you very much? Eventually some other poor fool will screw up and give the locals something else to talk about." The most difficult thing he'd had to deal with the past two months had been Molly's heartbreak. Although Macie had never been much of a mother, she had, in her own way, loved their child, and Molly had always harbored some hope that Macie would miraculously turn into the ideal mom.

"I'm sure you're right." Lydia jumped when the waiter set her iced tea on the table.

Wade couldn't help but notice how tense she was, and he wondered if it was because she was with him or because she was in an alien environment here at Lewey's. Or were her nerves simply shot, due to the ordeal she'd endured the past two months? A combination of all three, he decided. "Hey, my marriage ended years ago, yet it's been difficult for me to accept the fact that Macie's dead. I didn't even love her, and yet I've mourned her."

Lydia's eyes opened wide. She stared at him, amazed by his brutal honesty.

"She was the mother of my child," he said by way of explanation.

Lydia shook her head affirmatively and reached out for the glass of tea. Her hand trembled slightly when she touched the cool glass. "I didn't know that Tyler was...that he... he was unfaithful."

"You never suspected?"

"I wouldn't let myself."

Even though her marriage had been less than ideal, and she had begun to have serious doubts about its survival during the past year, Lydia was having a difficult time accepting the fact that her life as Tyler's wife was over. For four years she had devoted herself to becoming the consummate helpmate for a man destined to be the governor of Mississippi. She had given up her own budding career as an interior designer when she'd left Birmingham as Tyler's bride. Over the past four years, she had served as a hospital volunteer, as a school board member, as chairman of her church's benevolent society and as an officer in numerous local clubs and charities. She had patterned her life after her mother's. Joan Kidman was the perfect wife, the ideal helpmate to her second husband, a Houston industrialist. And Lydia had tried to be just such a woman. She had invested four years and all her emotional energy into becoming a politician's wife.

Wade sipped on his cold beer, watching Lydia Reid and longing to take her into his arms. He wanted to say something that would comfort her. He wanted to tell her that Macie had probably instigated whatever had happened between her and Tyler Reid. But it wouldn't be right to bad-mouth a woman who wasn't alive to defend herself.

Lydia crossed her legs at the ankles and folded her hands in her lap, sitting straight-backed and proper the way she'd been taught. "It must be terrible for your little girl to have lost her mother."

"She's a tough kid, a lot like her old man, but, yeah, it's been hard on Molly."

"I...I...I'm sorry."

"Even though Macie wasn't mother material, Molly loved her. Macie didn't really want a kid. She only had Molly to hang on to me." Did admitting the truth make him sound like a heartless bastard? he wondered.

"But she must have loved her own child." Lydia had longed for a baby several years ago, but now she was thankful that she hadn't given birth to Tyler Reid's child.

"Look, just about everybody around these parts knows that Macie and I haven't lived as husband and wife since Molly was just a baby... nearly six years."

"Why didn't the two of you divorce?"

"I didn't want to take a chance on losing Molly or having to give Macie any part of my farm. The place has been in my family for four generations."

"So you and your wife lived separate lives?" Lydia was trying to ask, discreetly, if Wade and Macie had agreed to one of those modern, open marriages.

"We lived separate lives once I found out that Macie was sleeping around. I'm not the kind of man who can share his woman. You can be sure I'll never let another woman put me in that kind of situation."

Lydia wet her bottom lip with her tongue and bit down gently. "Did you know about Tyler and Macie?"

Wade watched the movement of her little pink tongue as she nervously licked across her lip. He wanted to capture her tongue in his mouth, to cover her lips with a passionate kiss and find out how much fire lay buried beneath her cool exterior. Damn, he was a fool! "Yeah, I knew. A lot of people knew."

"And you didn't care?" Lydia's hazel eyes sparkled with golden green fire.

"I stopped caring what Macie did years ago." He leaned over slightly, resting his big hands on the table. "She'd done all the damage she could do to my pride long before she took up with your husband."

A strange moaning sound came from Lydia, and the depth of pain in that single utterance seemed to shock her as much as it hurt him. Wade reached across the table and took her trembling hands into his strong, steady ones. "I'm sorry. If I could change things, I would. Somehow...well, somehow, I feel responsible."

She stared at him and found herself lost in his warm brown eyes. There was so much caring, so much compassion in those dark eyes. "No. No, you mustn't feel that way. If anyone is at fault, I am. Undoubtedly I wasn't enough...enough woman for my husband."

Wade cursed under his breath and tightened his hold on Lydia's hands. "Tyler Reid was a damned fool if you ask me. Men like him—" He stopped abruptly when he heard her indrawn breath. "I'm sorry, I've got no right to say these things."

Lydia looked down where Wade's big hands completely covered her smaller ones. Why, she wondered, of all the people who had tried to comfort her in the past two months, was Wade Cameron able to make her feel warm and alive and cared for? "You and I share a sort of special bond, don't we?"

"Yeah, I suppose we do." He released her hands, knowing that if he didn't let her go, he might grab her up into his arms and kiss the breath out of her. He couldn't allow himself to lose control and embarrass her, cause her any more pain.

"The whole town is talking, you know." When she reached for her iced tea, she knocked over the glass.

Wade caught the toppling glass before the remaining tea spilled. Several ice cubes sloshed over the side and spread out over the tabletop. Using several paper napkins, he cleaned up the spill.

"That matters to you a great deal, doesn't it, what people think of you?" She was so different from Macie, who hadn't given a tinker's damn what anybody thought of her. And she was different from his mother, too, a woman who believed in minding her own business and expected everyone else to do the same.

"Yes, I suppose it does," Lydia admitted, remembering all the times her mother had said, *What on earth will people think?*

"Being the mayor's wife put you under a magnifying glass, didn't it?"

"Tyler had great expectations. The party planned to run him for state senator next term, and then, in a few years—"

"Governor. Yeah, I'd heard."

"He was only thirty-one, you know."

"Macie was twenty-seven."

I want you to hold me, she said silently, her eyes filled with longing. More than sixty long, endless days and nights of pain and uncertainty, and no one could ease the agony. If only Wade Cameron would take her in his big, strong arms and hold her, everything would be all right. She knew her reasoning didn't make any sense, but then neither did the raw new emotions this stranger evoked within her.

"I'm so sorry this had to happen," she said. "I'm especially sorry for your little girl."

He had to get out of there fast or he'd wind up making a fool of himself. It didn't make any sense. It had been years since he'd wanted a woman the way he wanted Lydia Reid. Hell, he'd never wanted Macie this bad.

"Are you all right?" she asked. "Is something wrong?"

Racking his brain for an excuse, any excuse to get away from her, Wade breathed a sigh of relief when he saw his brother Britt come through the door. "There's my brother. I guess he's ready to load up the feed over at Clement's and head back for the farm."

Quickly Wade downed the last of his beer, stood up and grabbed his Stetson. Lydia looked up at him and smiled. She didn't want their time together to come to an end. Although it was obvious that she and Wade had very little in common, she knew she'd found a kindred soul in the big, dark farmer. He understood, as no one else could, the misery she endured each day; the loneliness, the shame.

Lydia stood. "I'll walk back with you and pick up my Tropicana."

Britt Cameron walked over to where Lydia and Wade stood by the booth. "Tanya's gone on over to the church to talk to Brother Charles. Let's get that feed loaded and go get her."

"This is my brother, Britt," Wade said. "Despite the fact that his actions disprove it, Ma did try to teach him some manners."

The younger man frowned, took a deep breath and looked at Lydia. "Sorry, ma'am."

Lydia didn't think she'd ever seen such a hard-looking man. It wasn't just the fact that his face and neck were scarred or that his left hand appeared deformed and crippled. There was something so intense, so fierce in Britt Cameron that she instinctively took a step backward. "Nice to meet you," she said, lying. She doubted that anyone would think it *nice* to meet this big, brooding man.

Wade paid the cashier and walked out beside Lydia, careful not to touch her. Their trip back up the street to Clement's created more of a stir than their trip down to Lewey's. At least two or three people hovered just inside each shop window, and townsfolk on the sidewalk stopped and stared as Lydia, Wade and Britt passed by. Lydia tried to pretend the threesome hadn't become the object of everyone's curiosity, but the moment they stepped inside Clement's, she breathed a sigh of relief and leaned back against the door frame.

"I'm sorry about that," Wade said, longing to comfort her, but knowing how impossible it would be to help her through this without causing her undue embarrassment.

"What the hell did you two expect, parading up to Lewey's for the whole town to see?" Britt asked, his tone brisk and accusatory.

"Shut up," Wade hissed under his breath.

Lydia's face lost all color. She swayed slightly. Wade caught her by the arm, steadying her. "He's right," she said. "Macie and Tyler have been the talk of the town for the last two months. Now it seems that you and I are."

When she turned to go farther inside the store, he tightened his hold on her arm. "Lydia..."

"I have to go."

He released her. She took several tentative steps away, then turned around. "We...we can't...can't see each other again."

"Yeah, I know." He turned to Britt. "Let's get that feed loaded and go pick up Tanya. Ma should have supper ready by the time we get home."

Two

Lydia had thought long and hard about what she was doing. If she was making a mistake, so be it. For over two weeks she had given thoughtful consideration before acting on her instincts to seek out Wade Cameron.

She had received numerous phone calls after her encounter with Wade at Clement's Feed and Seed. Concerned friends and acquaintances had cautioned her about being seen with *that man* again. Although all the calls had irritated her, only one had been unforgettable. The voice on the other end had been muffled, indistinguishable, and it had warned her, in no uncertain terms, to stay away from Wade Cameron.

For sixteen days Lydia had remembered every word she and Wade had exchanged, every gesture, every look. She had sought comfort and compassion from others, but had found that their sympathy held no real depth and consisted of little true understanding. She'd called her mother in Houston twice. Once Joan had been in the middle of a dinner party, and once had been just leaving for her hairdresser's. Last weekend Lydia had driven to her brother's in Alabama and sought distraction by baby-sitting her three nephews. She had even accepted dinner invitations from Glenn Haraway and his mother—three times.

No one else could possibly understand the horrendous problem that plagued her, the tormenting question that remained unanswered, the single most important issue left unresolved. There was no one else except Wade Cameron who would tell her the complete truth about Tyler and Macie.

Oh, she knew there had been a sexual relationship and that they had both died as the result of a one-car crash. The local authorities had very quickly hushed up the fact that both driver and passenger had been legally drunk. Realistically Lydia knew that she shouldn't be so obsessed with finding out the details—the whens and wheres and, most of all, the whys. She had done everything within her power to be a good wife to Tyler, the perfect helpmate. She had forgiven him his selfishness and overlooked his immaturity. Despite her own better judgment, she had trusted him. Now that he was dead, now that there was nothing else to lose, she had to know. And only one person in Riverton was strong enough, caring enough, brave enough to tell her the truth. Only one person could possibly understand why she would want to know.

Lydia pulled her BMW into the circular drive in front of the two-story wooden farmhouse. Stepping outside onto the dusty ground, she hesitated briefly beside the open car door, wondering if perhaps she should have called first. Closing the door, she took a deep breath and admitted that she'd been afraid to phone, afraid Wade Cameron wouldn't want to see her.

Before she reached the steps leading to the wrap-around porch, Lydia saw a dark-haired child running beside the house. If the barefooted little girl hadn't been so femininely beautiful, she could easily have been mistaken for a boy. She wore ragged cut-off jeans and a white T-shirt and her curly hair was cropped short. When the child saw Lydia, she stopped and smiled.

"Hi, did you come to see Grandma?"

Lydia's heart stopped for a split second. The dark eyes looking up at her were so familiar, as were the black hair, the dimpled chin and the full lips. This had to be Molly Cameron. She was the spitting image of her father. A tiny, feminine replica. "As a matter of fact, I've come to see your father."

"He's down at the chicken houses," the little girl said, stirring the dirt beneath her feet with the long stick she held in her hand. "Does he know you're coming?"

"Well, no, but do you suppose he'd have time to see me?"

"I guess so. You want me to show you the way to the chicken houses?"

A large, furry dog waddled off the front porch and down the steps. Molly Cameron squatted, reached out and put her arms around the animal's neck. "You can go, too, Bear. But be real careful because Grandma said we gotta take care of you until the puppies are born."

Lydia realized the fat dog was pregnant and that Molly Cameron obviously loved the mother-to-be. "Her name's Bear?" Lydia asked, walking over to take a better look.

"Yeah." Molly laughed, the movement bouncing her short black curls. "She's part cocker spaniel, part Chow and part Sooner, Daddy says, but she looks sort of like a little bear."

Lydia laughed, too, amazed how friendly, how utterly charming Wade's daughter was. "She does remind me a bit of a fuzzy teddy bear."

"You can pet her," Molly said. "She likes you. See how she's wagging her tail?"

Lydia bent down to pet Bear, threading her long fingers through the thick, dusty pelt. "I've never had a dog. Does Bear belong to you?"

"She sure does, and so does Rawhide."

"Who's Rawhide?"

"He's Bear's husband. The father of the puppies."

Lydia smiled, enjoying her conversation with Molly immensely. "Is Rawhide part this and that, too?"

"Naw, he's a miniature collie. He used to belong to my Aunt Tanya before she married Uncle Britt. I think her first husband gave her Rawhide."

"Molly Cameron!" The throaty, female voice came from the porch where a short, obese woman stood, her hands on her broad hips. She was dressed in a pair of stained jeans, a large white apron and a purple polka-dotted blouse. A pair of green flip-flops protected her bare feet from the hot wooden floor.

Molly jumped up and ran onto the porch. "Grandma, this lady's here to see Daddy."

Lydia approached the steps, then stopped dead still when Ruthie Cameron's hard, cold stare confronted her. "Hello, Mrs. Cameron. I'm . . . I'm Lydia Reid."

"I know who you are," Ruthie said, walking to the edge of the porch.

"I was fixing to take her down to the chicken houses to find Daddy," Molly said.

"I don't think Mrs. Reid wants to go to the chicken houses." Ruthie gave Lydia a thorough inspection. "You run on down and tell your daddy he's got company up at the house."

Molly obeyed instantly. Lydia felt a bit awkward, uncertain whether or not she was welcome, but definitely certain that Ruthie Cameron made her nervous.

"Come on up and have a seat." Ruthie motioned toward one of the big white rockers sitting on the porch. "Or, if it's too hot out here for you, we can go inside, but there ain't no air-conditioning except in the kitchen."

"I'll be fine out here, thank you." Lydia moved slowly up the steps, then waited for Mrs. Cameron to take a seat in the swing before she sat down in the rocker.

"Sure am sorry about your husband." Ruthie untied the strings of the apron that covered her huge stomach, removed the garment and folded it on her lap. "It's hard on a woman without her man. My Hoyt died when Wade was just sixteen. Left me with four young'uns. Britt was fourteen and the girls were nine and eleven."

"How on earth did you manage?" Lydia couldn't imagine being widowed with four children and stuck on a farm.

"Wade took over. He grew up fast."

"I hope you don't mind that I've come out here." For some reason Lydia felt that she needed to explain why she wanted to see Wade. "Your son and I, through a strange set of circumstances, have found ourselves in a similar situation. There are things I need to discuss with him, things I haven't been able to discuss with anyone else."

"Ain't none of my business why you're here." Ruthie crossed her arms across her ample bosom.

"I promise that I haven't come here to make things more difficult for Wa...for your son."

"I believe you."

"I need his help to understand what happened to my life, why my husband was unfaithful to me." Lydia hadn't meant to blurt out her heartache that way, but the words escaped before she'd had time to stop them.

"Oh, gal, that's something you ain't gonna ever know. A man's either got it in him to be faithful or he ain't. You've probably been thinking it's something you did, and that's where you're wrong."

Tears stung Lydia's eyes. She closed her mouth tightly in an effort to keep from crying out. Ruthie Cameron had seen right through her, straight to her heart.

"Good afternoon, Mrs. Reid," Wade Cameron said as he came toward the porch.

Lydia looked out into the yard. He stood several feet away, his gaze riveted to her. His jeans were faded, torn and dirty. His dingy white T-shirt was filled with tiny holes. A day's growth of beard shadowed his rugged face, and bits of sawdust nestled in his black hair. Never had she seen a more welcome sight. She felt as if she'd been lost and now was found, as if she had walked out of darkness into the light of day. She wanted to run to him, throw herself into his arms and beg him to hold her and keep her safe.

"Hello, Mr. Cameron." Lydia stood up on legs that had suddenly become unsteady. She caught the arm of the rocker to balance herself. "I need a few minutes of your time. There . . . there's something I need to talk to you about."

Ruthie grasped her apron in one hand and used her other hand to boost her fat body up from the swing. "Come on, Molly. You can help me fix a peach cobbler for supper."

Molly ran up the steps. "Can I roll out the dough?"

"You sure can." Ruthie opened the screened door, then turned to smile at Lydia. "We had a bumper crop of peaches this year, Mrs. Reid. Before you leave, stop by the kitchen and I'll give you a basket to take home with you."

"Thank you. I'll do that." Lydia was baffled by Ruthie Cameron. She'd never known anyone like her, so countrified and plain and so completely outspoken and unconcerned with appearances. At first she'd thought Wade's mother disliked her, but now she didn't think so. The woman was a complete puzzle to Lydia, and yet she liked her. There was something about Ruthie Cameron that reminded Lydia of her Grandmother Milner. The resemblance wasn't physical, and certainly not in mannerisms or speech. Cleo Milner had been a well-educated, well-read and world-traveled woman, but she had possessed the same simple, down-to-earth attitude toward life that Ruthie Cameron did.

For endless minutes after Ruthie and Molly went inside, Lydia and Wade stood on the porch and stared at each other. The farm was miles away from town and acres from the nearest neighbor, so it contained only the sounds and sights and smells of nature. The sun lay low in the western sky, yet still cast a summery warmth and glow that would last several more hours until sundown.

Wade had practically run all the way from the chicken houses, leaving Britt cursing him for being a fool. His brother had loudly and vehemently warned Wade to stay away from Lydia Reid, had even suggested strongly that she would cause him more grief than Macie ever had. Of course Britt's own marital problems tended to cloud his judgment just a bit.

"You want to sit out here or go in the house?" Wade asked, wiping off his dirty hands on the sides of his tattered jeans.

"I . . . it doesn't matter." This had been a mistake, Lydia thought. It was obvious she had interrupted him in the middle of his work, and it was just as obvious that he wasn't overjoyed to see her.

"It's as cool out here as in the house, unless you want to join Ma and Molly in the kitchen. We rigged up an old air conditioner in there." Stuffing his hands into his back pockets, Wade shifted his feet. His gaze drifted over Lydia with what he hoped would appear to be indifference, then traveled over the porch as he tried not to look at her.

"It doesn't matter where we talk as long as we have some privacy." She wished he would look at her, really look at her. Then maybe she'd have some idea what he was feeling.

Damn, why did she have to look so good? he wondered. So cool and serene on this hot summer day. So fresh and clean, as if she'd just bathed and powdered. God, she smelled like flowers, the fragrance subtle yet overpowering to his senses.

"We could take a walk down to the spring," he suggested, nodding his head to the south. "Nobody's ever down there this time of day. It'll be about as private a place as you'll find on a working farm."

He waited for her to walk around him, then followed her down the steps and out into the yard. Watching her out of the corner of his eye, he took in every inch of her slender body encased in a sleeveless red jumpsuit. The garment fit snugly at the waist and was accented by a wide leather belt that matched her sandals. He couldn't help but realize how utterly out of place she looked on the farm.

As he led her around to the back of the house, she noticed the structure needed a fresh coat of paint and a few minor repairs. She couldn't be sure of the actual date the house had been built, but by its Victorian style, she guessed before the turn of the century. It was a huge old place—two stories, with a steep roof that probably concealed an enormous attic. A wrap-around porch covered the front, one side and part of the other side. The minimal amount of gingerbread trim was in remarkably good condition, all things considered.

"This is a lovely old house," she said, continuing to walk beside him without looking his way.

"My great-grandfather built it. There was a log house here before that. It burned."

After that brief bit of conversation, they walked in complete silence. Fat white clouds drifted along in the pale blue sky, while the sunshine spread its smile across fields planted in grain and soybeans. Far across in the eastern field, Lydia saw cattle grazing.

The farther he led her along the dirt path, the heavier the foliage, the thicker the trees. When they seemed surrounded by woods, a clearing appeared, and in the middle was a small pond, fed, Lydia supposed, by an underground spring. The first thing she noticed was how much cooler it had become, how quiet and still.

"This is beautiful."

"The water's not deep enough for a swim, but we used to play around in it when we were kids. Molly does now." Wade reached down and picked up a small broken limb.

"I appreciate your taking time out from your busy schedule to talk to me." She reached out and touched him on the arm and was surprised when he flinched and jerked away from her. "I'm sorry. Did I do something wrong?"

"No." He growled his answer. With nervous fingers he began stripping the leaves from the limb he held in his big hands.

"Perhaps I shouldn't have come here today." She looked up, then closed her eyes against the bright sunlight and tried to shut out the pain in her heart.

"Why did you?" He threw the bare limb to the ground.

This wasn't the way she'd thought it would be. She'd been so sure he would understand, so certain he would comfort her, that he would have the answers to her questions. She turned and began to walk away. "I'm sorry I bothered you."

Before she could take another step, he grabbed her, whirling her around so quickly her head began to spin. Staring up at him, she saw the fury in his black eyes, and suddenly felt afraid.

"Don't go," he said.

The tension in his big body was conspicuous. He glared at her, a visible twitch in the pulse in his neck. He relaxed his grip on her arms, but held her firmly away from him.

"It's obvious you don't want me here," she said.

"Lady, the problem is that I want you here too much, and you don't belong."

She didn't know how to respond, had never considered that his hostile attitude disguised a secret desire. She pulled away. He let her go. She brought her hands up to cover her mouth and nose, her fingertips resting under her eyes. Knowing she was close to tears didn't help Lydia's self-control.

"What do you want from me?" He closed his eyes, clenching his jaw and praying for the strength not to grab Lydia and lay her down on the soft grassy earth beneath their feet.

"I need to understand why Tyler was unfaithful to me. I have to know why he was having an affair with your wife." The words rushed out of her as if a dam had burst and the emotions could no longer be held back.

"And you thought I had the answers?" He shook his head and laughed, the sound a mixture of amazement and resentment. "I don't know a damn thing. If I had the answers to your questions, I could write a book and get rich."

"Your mother said that I'd never know. She . . . she believes some people have it in them to be faithful and some don't."

"Yeah, that sounds like Ma. A plain and simple answer to a complicated question."

"How did you live with the knowledge that your wife was unfaithful to you again and again? How did you ever stop picturing her with those men, seeing them together, knowing they had been intimate?" She refused to cry. She hadn't allowed herself to shed one tear since Tyler's death, and she had no intention of falling apart in front of Wade Cameron, whose whole attitude toward his late wife and marriage in general seemed so callous and unfeeling.

"At first I wanted to kill her." He couldn't bear to look at Lydia, see the agony on her face, the sorrow in her eyes. "After a while I stopped feeling anything. I became numb. I just didn't care what she did, or with whom."

"Oh, Wade."

"It took a lot longer before I could withstand the jeers and snide remarks other guys made about my wife. I got into more than one brawl because of it, even landed in jail a couple of times."

"Was there something special about Macie that made her so irresistible to men?"

Wade looked at her, amazed that a wealthy, well-educated lady like Lydia Reid could be so stupid when it came to the subject of men and women. "Yeah, there was something that made her irresistible to any man on the make. She was available."

Lydia stared at him as if she'd misunderstood what he'd said. "That's it?"

"You want me to tell you that Macie made the move on your husband, that she went after him? Okay. Macie probably made the offer. A guy like Tyler Reid would have been a challenge to her. He was a rich boy on his way up the ladder of success, and he was way out of her league.''

Lydia didn't want to hear any more. She knew what Wade was going to say next. "She wasn't the first."

"Of course she wasn't the first, and she wouldn't have been the last."

Lydia put her hands over her ears as if the gesture could block out the truth, could erase the ugly reality she had to face. "Why wasn't I enough? Why? Why?"

In one swift move, Wade grabbed her, pulling her into his arms, forcing her head onto his chest. Moving his big hands up and down her back, he stroked her as her body trembled. More than anything he wished he could answer her question, but he couldn't. He had no idea what had prompted Tyler Reid's infidelity. More than likely, Ma's homespun philosophy was as close to the truth as a person could get.

Wade tilted Lydia's face upward so that they were staring directly at each other. He tightened his hold on her quivering chin. "You're going to have to realize that there's nothing wrong with you, that your husband wasn't unfaithful because you weren't woman enough to hold him. Take my word for it, lady, a man would kill for the right to make love to you."

"Oh . . ." His words soothed her, a balm to her tortured heart. Nothing he could have said would have affected her so deeply or frightened her so badly. She'd never been with a man other than her husband, but at this very minute the thought of Wade Cameron taking her, making love to her, filled her mind with steamy images of the two of them lying naked in the grass beside the spring.

He could see the desire in her eyes, could feel the increase in her heartbeat. Damn it to hell, but he wanted her. Releasing her chin, he ran his hand down her throat, down her chest, stopping on the rise of her breasts. With his other hand he grabbed the back of her head and shoved her mouth against his, wet and hot and hard. She struggled momentarily, then opened her mouth, allowing him to enter her, taste her, conquer her.

God, she tasted sweet. Wild and sweet and hot. He moved his hand down to cup one firm breast while he ravaged her mouth. When she moaned, his lips ate the sound, devouring her wanton cry.

Suddenly Lydia began struggling, trying to push him away. Lost to the desire he felt, it took Wade several minutes to realize that she wanted him to stop, that she was fighting him. He released her. She jerked away from him, her eyes wild with desire yet filled with fear.

"It's all right, Lydia. It's all right." He reached out for her, but she moved backward.

"No, it's not. This was wrong. We had no right... no right..."

"It was my fault. I lost control." He'd wanted to comfort her, to love her, to prove to her what a desirable woman she was, but instead he'd made her feel cheap and used.

"I... I won't ever bother you again. I promise." As she spoke she began walking away. Stopping briefly, she looked over her shoulder. "And you'll leave me alone, won't you?"

Damn her! He'd never wanted anything the way he wanted Lydia Reid, and she was asking him not to see her again. "Yeah, I'll leave you alone."

Lydia ran up the dirt pathway, away from the quiet secluded spot where she'd completely lost control and been tempted to give herself to a man she barely knew.

Somehow, some way, she had to make sure that she and Wade Cameron never saw each other again. They could only bring each other more pain and sorrow, and she thought they'd both had enough to last a lifetime.

Three

The annual Founders' Day picnic was in full swing by the time Wade and his family arrived. He'd tried to get out of going, but Molly had refused to leave the farm without him.

Lydia Reid was sure to be there, and he knew he was sure to see her. He had no doubt that she'd been sitting in a place of honor up on the speaker's podium when the new mayor, former councilman Glenn Haraway, made the opening speech. By delaying his family's departure, Wade had at least been able to spare himself that ordeal.

From the size of the crowds milling around the town square, Wade figured half the county must be in attendance. Food vendors had set up booths on all four corners of the park area and in every available space on the sidewalks. Most of the shop windows displayed a scene from Riverton's past and numerous costumed reenactors played out miniscenes at various establishments and several outside locations. The smell of cotton candy blended with the hardier aroma of Southern barbecue.

The smoldering July sun dominated the day, its humid heat overpoweringly heavy. Wade noticed that most people's faces were flushed and damp with perspiration, their clothes spotted with moisture. Not even a hint of a breeze eased the smothering warmth. No relief could be found from the ninety-six-degree temperature, not even under the numerous shade trees in the square where so many celebrators had spread quilts and were sharing picnic lunches.

"It's so hot I wish I'd stayed home," Tanya Cameron said, repeatedly tugging on the front of her turquoise T-shirt in an effort to fan herself.

"Aw, Aunt Tanya, forget about the heat and look at all the fun things," Molly said, running around and around the four adults, slipping between them, bobbing up and down in front of and behind them.

"Britt, honey, let's go down to the Palace and get some ice cream." Tanya slipped her arm around her husband's waist.

"I'll take you in a few minutes. I promise. I just want to take a look at those hand-tooled leather belts over there first." Britt patted his wife on the shoulder.

"I'm going to die from this heat," Tanya said.

Ruthie Cameron grunted, gave her daughter-in-law a sharp look and walked ahead of them toward a booth filled with country craft items.

Wade knew his mother was as tired of seeing Tanya manipulate Britt as he was, but his brother's marriage was none of their business. Besides, he had problems of his own—and the biggest problem was standing only a few yards away.

Since the day she'd come to the farm, the day she'd sought him out for compassion and understanding and had gotten a heavy dose of passion, Wade had sworn that he'd never go anywhere near her again. But in reality he knew that sooner or later their paths were bound to cross. Maybe he'd hoped they would.

Even in this oppressive heat, she looked beautiful, Wade thought. Not quite so cool and aloof as usual, but every bit as appealing. She wore khaki walking shorts, a red sleeve-less blouse and matching tennis shoes. She'd pulled her shoulder-length brown hair up into a loose ponytail held atop her head with a gold clasp. Small gold hoops adorned her ears and a thin gold chain circled her throat.

She was with Glenn Haraway and an older woman, whose bright red hair suggested that she was probably the new mayor's mother. When he noticed Haraway slip his arm around Lydia's shoulder, Wade felt a surge of jealousy rip through him. He had recognized the signs of desire in Har-away's actions that night at the hospital, and it was obvi-ous that his intentions toward Lydia were sexual. Was she aware that ol' friend-of-the-family wanted to bed her?

"Look, Daddy, there's Mrs. Reid," Molly said. "Can I go say hi?"

"No." Wade's answer was quick and harsh.

"Your daddy don't want you bothering Mrs. Reid while she's talking to her friends." Ruthie Cameron patted the child on the head. "Me and you'll make our way over to see her before we leave."

"I hear folks are saying that the new mayor's mama wants to see him married to the widow Reid once a proper amount of time has passed," Tanya said. "I guess everybody thinks me and Britt got married too soon after Paul's death."

Wade had no intention of hearing all that garbage again, and didn't see how his brother endured the guilt trip Tanya kept them both on. "Come on, Britt, let's go take a look at those belts."

"Wait, Daddy, Mrs. Reid and her friends are coming over here," Molly said, jumping up and down. "See, she's looking at us." Molly waved and Lydia Reid waved back at her.

Lydia thought she might faint, but knew she didn't dare give in to the weakness, even if it would be a way to get out of having to speak to Wade Cameron.

"Come on, Lydia," Glenn said, trying to pull her forward. "I want to catch up with the Camerons before they get lost in this crowd."

"You two go along and talk business to that bunch," Eloise said, tilting her nose upward just a fraction as if she smelled something unpleasant. "I've got to get over to the library. My reading is at two-thirty."

"We'll meet you later, Mother."

"Good luck with that old Cameron woman." Eloise snorted, the sound a mixture of disgust and superiority. "She's so ignorant, she can't comprehend what a new mall would mean to Riverton."

Lydia had to bite her tongue to keep from defending Ruthie Cameron, but she didn't dare. Eloise would never understand why and would probably question her motives. How could she explain to someone with Eloise's breeding that the world would be better off with a few more hardworking, down-to-earth people like Wade Cameron's mother?

Lydia allowed Glenn to lead her across the few yards of green grass that separated them from the Cameron family. She tried not to look at Wade, but her eyes didn't cooperate. He was wearing his customary faded jeans, scuffed boots and cotton shirt, but the Stetson was missing. His black hair gleamed like ebony silk, not a hint of brown showed even in the glare of the summer sun. No one looking at this man would doubt he spent a great deal of his time outdoors. His skin was deeply tanned, and faint lines edged the corners of his mouth and eyes ... his beautiful brown eyes....

"Good afternoon, Mrs. Cameron." Glenn extended his hand, a politician's smile on his face.

Ruthie Cameron glanced down at the mayor's hand, then up at his face. "It was."

"Look here, Haraway, if you've come over here to pester Ma about selling her property on Cotton Row, then you can leave." Britt glared at Glenn, whom he towered over by a good six inches.

Ruthie reached out and shook Glenn's hand. "You take Tanya on over to the Palace, boy. I can talk for myself."

Lydia watched Britt's reaction. She expected anger and annoyance, but he surprised her. Britt laughed, put his arm around his petite blond wife and headed off in the direction of the local drugstore and ice-cream parlor.

"Mrs. Cameron, if you'd just give me a chance to explain all the benefits, not only to Riverton but to your family, as well, of selling that property over on Cotton Row, I'm sure you'd agree to see things the city council's way."

Glenn Haraway didn't have Tyler Reid's devastating, movie-star looks, but he did have that same ready smile and silver tongue, Lydia thought as she listened to his little speech.

"I done told you, more than once, that I got no intention of selling." Ruthie crossed her arms over her bosom and leaned back, eyeing Glenn with a suspicious glare.

"What can I say or do to make you see reason?" Glenn asked, a slight edge to his voice.

"Not a damned thing." Ruthie turned around and walked away, leaving Glenn staring, open-mouthed and bug-eyed.

Lydia couldn't suppress a tiny grin, thinking how unaccustomed Glenn must be to hearing someone's mother curse. Ladies, like Eloise Haraway and her peers, were far too refined for such language.

Wade saw the corners of Lydia's mouth turn upward and realized that she'd found his mother's reply humorous instead of offensive. He wasn't sure why, but that notion pleased him and gave him a new insight into the lady's personality.

"Mrs. Reid?" Molly tugged on Lydia's hand and was rewarded by a smile.

"Hello, Molly, how are you today?" Lydia noticed that Wade's daughter, though absolutely adorable, still could easily pass for a pretty little boy. She wore cut-off jeans, a

Braves T-shirt and scuffed Nikes without any socks. *If she were my little girl*, Lydia thought—then stopped herself abruptly. Thinking like that could be dangerous.

"I'm hot, that's how I am," Molly said, then motioned Lydia to bend over by curling her index finger and staring up beseechingly.

Lydia leaned down. "What is it?"

"I don't think Grandma likes your friend."

Lydia laughed, then whispered, "I think you're right."

"Molly, it isn't polite to whisper," Wade said.

"It's not polite to hurt someone's feelings, either," the child replied.

Glenn tugged on Lydia's arm. "There's Senator Biddle. I've got to catch him before he leaves."

"By all means." Lydia pulled free from Glenn's grasp. "You go ahead. I'll meet you and Eloise later."

"Lydia, I really don't think—"

"She said she'd meet you later," Wade said.

"See here, Cameron—"

"People are watching us," Lydia said, knowing that that particular statement would cease Glenn's protests.

"Don't be long, my dear." Glenn left, practically running to catch up with the state senator who was in town to celebrate Riverton's annual Founders' Day.

Lydia tried to concentrate all her attention on Molly, but she kept stealing glances at Wade. He was watching her intently, a glint of humor in his dark eyes.

"Bear had her puppies," Molly said. "Seven of 'em. You want one, Mrs. Reid?"

"Oh, my, Molly, I don't know." Lydia had never owned a dog, although she loved animals. Her mother had considered pets nasty, and when Lydia had lived on her own, she hadn't wanted to coop up a dog in her Birmingham apartment. Of course, Tyler had shared her mother's opinion of pets.

"Molly's trying to find good homes for all of Bear's babies. We've got three more to go." Wade ruffled the curls atop his daughter's head.

Lydia envied what she could see was a close and loving relationship between Wade and his child. Once, years ago, she'd been that close to her own father. His death from an unexpected heart attack when she was twelve had been the first tragedy in Lydia's life.

"You know, I think I just might like to have one of Bear's puppies. Do you have a boy left?" Lydia was so glad that she wasn't facing Wade alone, that she had the buffer of his precious little girl to come between them and the inevitable tension they generated.

"Oh, Daddy, let's give her the tawny, scrawny lion one." Molly giggled as she hopped up and down.

"He's not really scrawny, but he does look like a lion. The tawny, scrawny bit comes from one of Molly's storybooks," Wade explained. "Don't feel obligated to take one of the pups if you don't really want one."

Lydia looked at him, and feelings so warm and sweet filled her that she almost cried. Wade Cameron was a multifaceted man. A hard-working farmer. A steadfast son. A loving father. An incredibly sexy hunk. If only she had met him years ago. Before Tyler. Or even sometime in the future when she wasn't under twenty-four-hour-a-day surveillance by the whole town.

"I can send someone out to the farm to pick him up when he's old enough to be weaned from Bear." Lydia knew she could never go through a repeat performance of making a trip out to the Cameron farm. The first experience had been more than enough to keep her away forever.

"Oh, no, we'll bring him by your house," Molly said. "Won't we, Daddy?"

"If it's all right with Mrs. Reid."

She realized that there was no way to get out of the situation without hurting Molly's feelings. Besides, what harm would it do for Wade and his daughter to stop by her house for a few minutes to bring the puppy?

"I'll be looking forward to it. And I definitely want the tawny, scrawny lion puppy." Lydia knew that Wade was staring at her, but she refused to acknowledge his scrutiny. "I'm afraid I've got to be going. We're expected at the country club for drinks in a little while."

Wade stood on the sidewalk in the middle of the town square and watched Lydia Reid walk away. For a few minutes she had seemed like any other woman—warm, friendly, approachable. He'd enjoyed seeing how well she and Molly got along and had felt a sense of relief that he and Lydia had been able to act so naturally with each other after their last wild encounter. But her parting comment had brought him back to reality. He was on his way to buy his daughter a corn dog. Lydia Reid was on her way to the country club for drinks.

Lydia was glad that she wouldn't have to go through this day again. Despite the fact that it had been a little over four months since Tyler's death, she had just today forced herself to go through his belongings, pack away items she could no longer bear to look at and sack all his clothes into Goodwill bags.

Even though Tyler's death had caused her more than the normal amount of grief a widow would feel, she had begun to put their shared life and their sham of a marriage into the proper perspective. Everything hadn't been Tyler's fault. If she hadn't been so intent on becoming a carbon copy of her mother, she would have allowed herself to suspect the truth long before she did. Tyler had used her. But she had let him.

Looking to make sure that Glenn and Eloise were nowhere in sight, Lydia pushed open the sliding glass doors and stepped down onto the patio. A slight evening breeze brushed across her face, and she breathed in the heady fragrance of her rose garden, which was in full bloom. It was almost eight o'clock, but due to daylight savings time it would be almost another hour before night fell in Mississippi.

She sat down in the wooden glider on the patio, leaned her head back against the cushions and let out a deep sigh. A late-afternoon rain had temporarily cooled the August heat, but had left behind a steamy residue. She checked her watch for the fifth time in the last five minutes. They should arrive at any time, she thought. Molly had called thirty minutes ago to see if tonight would be a good time to bring the tawny, scrawny puppy to his new home.

Lydia kept telling herself that it was ridiculous to be so nervous. After all, what could possibly happen with Molly present? Wade was hardly likely to say or do anything that would be the least bit suggestive. But that fact hadn't kept Lydia's imagination from going into overdrive. It was amazing how many torrid, sensuous scenes could race through a woman's mind in thirty minutes.

The sound of a truck coming into the drive brought Lydia out of her dazed thoughts. She heard a door slam and Molly's childish laughter. Slowly, calmly, Lydia walked over to the fence and opened the gate, allowing Wade and his daughter to enter her backyard.

Just the sight of him gave Lydia butterflies in her stomach and heart palpitations. Every time she saw him she wanted to walk into his arms and ask him to keep her safe forever. Looking at him standing there with a shaggy gold and white puppy in his arms, she wondered if the man owned any clothing other than jeans and cotton shirts.

"We brought Leo," Molly said, reaching up to take the dog from her father. "If you don't like the name we've given him, you can change it, but he already answers to Leo."

"Leo, huh?" Lydia inspected the hairy animal rooting around in Molly's plump little arms. "Leo the Lion. It suits him with that mane of golden hair."

"You gonna keep him out here?" Molly asked, looking around the large wood-enclosed backyard. "Or are you letting him stay inside some, too? Grandma won't let me keep

Bear and Rawhide in the house. Says animals weren't meant to be kept inside."

"Well, I suppose your grandmother has a point," Lydia said. "But I think Leo might like inside as much as outside." And he'll be so much company for me, she thought. A warm, caring companion. Someone who'd depend on her for his every want. Someone who'd love her.

"Well, Molly, we've delivered Leo, and I'm sure Mrs. Reid has other things to do—" Wade said.

"Do we have to leave already?" Molly frowned, puckering up her round little face into a snarl.

"No, of course you don't," Lydia heard herself saying, and couldn't believe she was stupid enough to insist that Wade Cameron stay one minute longer than necessary.

"See, Daddy, Mrs. Reid wants us to stay."

"Molly, I'd like for you to call me Lydia, if it's all right with your father. After all, we're friends and friends should be on a first-name basis, don't you think?"

"What does that mean, first-name basis?" Molly blinked as if she were contemplating some serious mathematical equation.

"It just means that instead of our saying Mrs. Reid and Miss Cameron, we'll say Lydia and Molly."

"Am I Miss Cameron?" Molly asked, looking up at her father.

"Yep." Wade smiled over his daughter's head at Lydia. Damn, she was good with Molly. Warm. Caring. Understanding. All the things a mother should be.

"Can I see inside your house?" Molly turned to Lydia.

"Molly Sue Cameron!" Wade shouted.

"Come on in," Lydia said, laughing, as much at Wade's outraged cry as Molly's impudence. "I'll give you a grand tour. And bring Leo. He might as well sniff out his new surroundings."

"He's liable to start marking his territory." Wade laughed, then followed Lydia and his daughter into the house.

"No doubt." Lydia led them into her den. "All male animals are territorial, aren't they? I'll just have to keep a mop, a scoop and plenty of Lysol on hand."

For the next hour, Lydia entertained the Camerons by giving them a complete tour of the house and even serving cake and iced tea. When they had noticed all the boxes scattered throughout the house, she'd had to explain about packing away Tyler's possessions. Molly had said that Grandma had done that with her mother's things right after Macie's funeral, and that her daddy had given her some of her mother's things for keepsakes.

The most awkward moment had come when she found herself alone in her bedroom with Wade. Molly and Leo had taken a bathroom break. Neither she nor Wade spoke. They stood, each on opposite sides of her canopy bed, and stared at each other. The moments seemed like hours while they waited for Molly to join them again.

Images formed in her mind, so vivid that Lydia blushed from their clarity. She could almost feel Wade's arms around her, his lips touching hers, his big, hard body bearing down and into her. Thankfully Molly rejoined them just as Wade walked around the bed.

Once the refreshments had been served and consumed, Wade insisted they leave, and Molly reluctantly agreed.

"Why don't you bring Leo out to the farm sometime, Mrs. er...Lydia? You could come eat supper with us," Molly said, stepping down onto the patio.

Lydia looked at Wade, seeking an affirmation. Was he willing to offer the same invitation? The blank stare he gave her told Lydia nothing, and she realized that he wasn't going to make the first move. "Thank you for inviting me. I promise I'll think about a visit."

"Come on, curly top," Wade said, swinging his daughter up on his hip.

"Bye, Lydia. Bye, Leo." Molly waved, and continued waving until after she and Wade got in the truck and pulled out of the driveway.

Lydia suddenly felt more alone than she'd felt in months. A part of her had wanted Wade and Molly Cameron to stay, to become a part of her life, to fill the emptiness in her heart. But that wasn't possible, and there was no point in dreaming of something that could never be.

At her feet Leo whimpered. She knelt down, picked him up and turned to go back inside the house when the gate opened and Eloise Haraway walked into the backyard.

"Was that Macie Cameron's husband?" Eloise asked, her faded blue eyes wide and inquiring.

"That was Wade Cameron and his daughter Molly." Lydia didn't know if she could endure her neighbor's curiosity.

"What on earth were they doing coming to see you? I must say I think it terribly unfeeling of that Cameron man to visit you, for whatever reason. He must know that seeing him would only remind you of Tyler's... well, Tyler's little indiscretion."

"His daughter's dog had pups and they brought me one." Cuddling Leo in her arms, Lydia stroked his head.

"So I see. But why?"

"Because I'd asked for one when Glenn and I talked to them on Founders' Day."

"Oh, my dear, you should have insisted that Glenn come over while they were here, then there could have been no hint of scandal."

"You don't think a six-year-old child is a proper chaperon?"

"Well, yes, I suppose." Eloise moved to Lydia's side and whispered, "You aren't planning on seeing him again, are you?"

Lydia tried not to smile. More than anything she wanted to tell Eloise Haraway that it was none of her business whether or not she planned to see Wade again. Of course, she couldn't say that. She was, after all, a lady with a reputation to uphold. "No, Eloise, I have no plans to see Mr. Cameron again."

"Good. Good." Eloise smiled, patted Lydia on the back and followed her inside the house.

By eleven o'clock that night, Lydia had showered and changed into a pair of royal-blue silk lounging pajamas. She'd found a Clint Eastwood Western on Channel Eight and had just settled down on the couch when she heard a truck enter her driveway. Instinctively she knew Wade Cameron had returned. She knew because, subconsciously, she'd been wishing that he'd come back.

Taking a deep, calming breath, she walked over to the double glass doors and turned on the backyard light, then pushed the doors open and stepped down onto the patio. Wade was standing at the open gate, wearing the same clothes he'd worn earlier.

With his little tail wagging a friendly hello, Leo ran straight to the tall, dark man whose shadow fell across Lydia's rose garden as he began walking toward the house.

"Mr. Cameron?" Lydia wanted to ask him why he was here, but somehow it didn't matter. She was simply glad to see him.

"I hope you don't mind that I—" He looked down at his feet—big feet clad in Western-style leather boots. "I think we need to talk."

"Won't you come in?" Glancing outside the gate, she caught a glimpse of a mud-splattered blue truck parked in her driveway, and then she noticed a slight movement in Eloise Haraway's kitchen window.

Wade followed her inside to the tidy den. An overstuffed Colonial sofa and matching chair dominated the small room. White Priscilla curtains adorned the windows and elaborate cross-stitched pictures covered the walls.

"I guess I shouldn't be here," he said, "but I can't stop thinking about you . . . about us."

"I'm glad you came back, Mr. Cameron." She led him farther into the room. "Please sit down." She indicated the sofa and then seated herself in a nearby Boston rocker.

"Thanks." He rested his long, lean frame on the cushiony sofa, placing his hands on top of his muscular legs. "Under the circumstances, do you suppose you could call me Wade?"

"Wade." He seems as nervous as I am, she thought. But then, perhaps he was only a bit uncomfortable. She couldn't help noticing, once again, what an attractive man Wade Cameron was, sitting there so big and dark and completely male.

Neither of them spoke for what seemed to Lydia like hours, nor could they bring themselves to look at each other. Finally Lydia asked, "May I get you something to drink? I'm certain there's coffee left, or would you prefer something else?"

"Nothing, thanks." Dammit he was a fool! He had no business being here, and he knew it. He hadn't been able to stop thinking about her, once he and Molly had gotten back to the farm. He'd argued with himself for hours, finally losing the fight. All the way here he'd tried to prepare his speech. He wanted to offer her friendship—just friendship. Lydia Reid was a lady who'd be scared off if he told her, outright, what he really wanted. However, he didn't fool himself into thinking she wouldn't be aware of his true motives.

"The whole town is talking, you know." She got up and walked over to the windows facing the Haraway home next door. "Right now Eloise Haraway is watching, hoping she'll see something. Regardless of what she does or doesn't see, she'll be on the phone bright and early tomorrow morning telling anyone who'll listen that a truck was parked in my driveway at nearly midnight, and that handsome Cameron man was paying a visit."

"You think I'm handsome?"

"Wade..."

"I think you're just about the most beautiful thing I've ever seen."

"Please don't."

He shifted his big body, moving closer to the edge of the couch. Closer to Lydia. "You're worried about your reputation."

"My husband has been dead four months. It's hardly appropriate for me to be entertaining men at my home so late at night." Lydia caught the lapels of her pajama top in her fingers, twisting the soft material into a wad.

"I want us to be friends," he said, standing up abruptly.

"Friends?" She stared at him with wide eyes, not quite believing what he'd said.

"I think we'd be good for each other. We sort of understand . . . well, I mean we're in the same boat. Your husband. My wife."

"There's more between us than that, Wade." Lydia knew they had to address her worse fears before there was any chance they could share a friendship. "We're . . . we're sexually attracted to each other."

"Damn!"

"I'm not ready for a relationship with a man. This is August. Tyler died in April. Don't you see how unseemly—"

"You think you have to be faithful to the memory of a man who didn't know the meaning of the word?" Wade raked his fingers through his hair, mussing the already unruly curls.

"I have to be true to my own morals," Lydia said, standing up and walking over to place her hand on Wade's arm.

He jerked around and glared at her. "Can't we try friendship?"

"Our seeing each other alone, even under the most innocent of circumstances, is bound to cause a lot of talk."

"May Molly and I stop by for a visit next Saturday?"

"I . . . yes. Yes, I'd like that very much."

"I guess I'd better be going," he said and turned to leave. Hell, he didn't want to go. He wanted to grab her, throw her down on the couch and make hot, wild love to her.

She followed him to the door. "Thank you for coming by, Wade. For offering me your friendship."

"It may not work."

"But we'll give it a try, won't we, Wade?"

He loved the sound of his name on her lips, the soft breathless way she said it. He wondered how she'd say it when they made love.

He bent his head, and with a tremendous amount of willpower, kissed her on the cheek. His entire body went rigid. His erection strained against his tight jeans.

He pulled away from her, stepped down onto the patio and turned around to face her. "Look, if you ever need anything..."

"Thank you, Wade."

"Take care, huh?"

She walked out onto the patio and watched him get in his truck and back out of her driveway for the second time tonight. Just as she turned to reenter the house, Lydia caught a glimpse of Eloise Haraway standing on her back steps, her hair curled on pink rollers, and her tall body draped in a cotton housecoat. Well, Lydia thought, there was no doubt about it. By tomorrow, Wade Cameron's visit to the widow Reid would be the talk of the town.

Four

Wade popped the last bite of biscuit into his mouth and washed it down with black coffee. Sunday was the only day he allowed himself the luxury of a leisurely breakfast.

Leaning back in the wooden chair, he crossed his booted feet under the old kitchen table and picked up the *Riverton Chronicle*. His mother and daughter had already gutted the newspaper. He had spent a good fifteen minutes reading the comics to Molly while Ruthie Cameron scanned the sales papers.

Glenn Haraway and Lydia Reid stared at him from the front page of the *Chronicle*. Even with her long hair pulled back from her face into a bun, and dressed in a dark suit, she was beautiful. The very thought of her conjured up images of warm, pink lips and soft, moist skin. Somehow he had allowed Tyler Reid's widow to become a fever in his blood, a fever with only one cure.

Wade knew how difficult it had been for Lydia to watch another man move into her husband's office, even though she had no doubts that former councilman Glenn Haraway would make an excellent mayor. Wade knew how she felt because he'd seen Lydia once a week for the past six weeks, usually with Molly acting as chaperon. He'd made a point of getting into town every Saturday afternoon, and Lydia always welcomed him and his child into her den where they shared a few hours of companionship. Being Lydia's friend was the most difficult thing Wade had ever done. He wanted to be her friend, but, by God, he wanted to be more, so much more.

He never said why he came and she never asked. While Molly played with Leo or busied herself with Lydia's doll collection, he and Lydia talked. At first, they talked about Tyler and Macie, and then they began talking about themselves. He learned that she'd been very close to her father, an Alabama circuit court judge, and that his death, when she was twelve, had devastated her. She had a warm and cordial relationship with her millionaire stepfather, and she and her social butterfly mother spoke often on the phone, but seldom visited each other. Her lawyer brother lived in Alabama with his wife and three children.

Lydia had obtained a master's degree from the University of Alabama and had operated her own interior design firm in Birmingham when she met Tyler Reid. The third-generation Mississippi politician had been searching for just the right wife, and he'd found the perfect woman in Lydia Lee Milner.

Although Wade had garnered a great deal of personal information about her during their conversations, he knew relatively little about the intimate side of her marriage. Then again, he hadn't told her a damn thing about his sex life, either.

"Molly's riding in to church with Tanya this morning," Ruthie Cameron said as she entered the kitchen.

"You're not going today?" Wade asked, looking up from the newspaper.

His mother was old before her time. Her life hadn't been an easy one, and it showed on her wrinkled face and stooped shoulders. At fifty-two, she could easily be mistaken for a woman in her late sixties. She wore her muddy-gray hair cropped boyishly short, and never once had Wade seen her in more makeup than lipstick. She stood barely two inches over five feet and, though fifty pounds overweight, she could work rings around most younger, slimmer women. Ruthie Cameron was a country woman, born and raised on a Mississippi farm, and given her own way she would die working in her vegetable garden.

"Arthritis in my foot's acting up a bit." Ruthie began running water into the sink.

"Britt's not going to church, either?" Wade asked.

"You know he don't like that new preacher. Says he ain't going back as long as that so-and-so's there."

"Could he be jealous?" Wade had hoped that his brother's marriage would fare better than his own had. But since both of them had married for the wrong reasons, he doubted Britt's marriage had any better chance of succeeding than his had. "Tanya seems quite taken with Brother Charles. I hear he's good-looking and single."

"Don't talk such nonsense," Ruthie said, a frown marring her wrinkled forehead. "Besides, your brother's marriage is none of my business."

"Neither is my love life."

Ruthie squirted dishwashing detergent into the water, then took an apron from a nearby drawer and tied it around her thick waist. "I ain't being nosy, son. The things I've said to you were said out of concern for you and for Lydia Reid. How are you two going to handle the situation if it gets out of control, tell me that?"

"There's nothing to tell, Ma." Wade folded the paper and laid it on the table.

Ruthie gathered up the dirty dishes and slipped them into the dishwater. "You ain't said a word to me about what's going on between you and Mrs. Reid."

"What do you want me to say about her?"

"I usually mind my own business, but... well, I sure would hate to see you get hurt again, son." Ruthie ran a dishcloth over a soiled plate. "And even though I don't really know Lydia Reid, I'd say she's had about all the sorrow she can stand. You don't want to cause her any more pain, do you?"

"What are you talking about?" Wade stood up, pushing the chair backward with his legs.

"I don't normally listen to gossip. It's a waste of time. But when my oldest son is the one people are whispering about, I listen."

Wade walked across the room to the coffeepot and poured himself another cup. "Well, go ahead and tell me what they're saying."

"They say you're sniffing around Tyler Reid's widow." Ruthie turned her dark brown eyes toward her son.

"I've stopped by a few times to check on her. There's nothing more to it." Wade put his hand on his mother's plump shoulder. "I have no intention of getting involved with Lydia Reid or any other woman. I plan on staying single the rest of my life."

"Folks are saying her high-class friends ain't none too pleased about you and her seeing each other."

"We're not seeing each other!"

"No need for you to raise your voice to me, boy. I ain't accusing you of nothing. You're a grown man." Ruthie lifted the dishes from the rinse water and began stacking them on the drain rack.

"She needs a friend right now. Someone she can talk to." Wade laid his head on top of his mother's and hugged her tightly. "And I need somebody, too."

"You've needed somebody for a long time, and that's what's got me worried." Ruthie dried her hands on her apron and slid her arm around her son's waist.

"After all these years, are you finally getting around to giving me that sex talk parents are supposed to give their children?" he asked, smiling.

"I ain't talking about a roll in the hay. I'm talking about love."

Wade laughed and gave his mother another tight hug before retrieving his coffee cup and sitting back down at the table. "That's one thing you don't have to worry about. I'm immune to love. Macie cured me of that ailment."

"Well, mark my words, son, you got just about as much control over love as you do the weather. So you best watch out or you'll get yourself caught up in a tornado."

"We're having a tornado?" Molly Cameron asked as she walked into the kitchen. Her short black curls framed an angelic face, and deep dimples marked her cheeks when she smiled at her father.

"The only tornadoes around here are in your grandma's head," Wade assured his daughter as he lifted her up onto his lap. "You sure do look pretty today. Is that a new dress?"

"Grandma made it for me." Molly lifted the hem of her plain pink gingham dress.

A car horn blew outside the Cameron house. Molly jumped from her father's lap and made a mad dash for the back door where Wade's sister-in-law waited. "Bye. See y'all after church."

"She's awfully excited about church today," Wade said.

"They're giving gold stars for attendance now." Ruthie poured herself a cup of coffee and sat down beside her son.

"She seems to be doing fine without Macie, doesn't she?"

"She did fine without Macie when Macie was alive. You and I both know I've raised that child. But she needs a mama, someone a lot younger than me. Someone who can teach her what girls need to know about these days."

"I suppose you have someone in mind, don't you?" Wade asked.

"There's quite a few good country girls who'd be proud to marry up with you. And that's what you need, a gal who grew up out here and knows what our life is like."

"If you're worried that I've got any notions about marrying Lydia Reid, you can set your mind to rest. A lady like her wouldn't have an old farm boy like me."

"Please thank Eloise again for a lovely lunch," Lydia said as she inserted the key in the lock of her front door.

"Mother is terribly fond of you, you know," Glenn said, standing directly behind Lydia as she opened the door.

She turned to face her attentive escort. "And thank you for the lovely afternoon ride. With November almost here, this beautiful autumn foliage won't last much longer."

"It was my pleasure, I assure you." Glenn followed her into the foyer.

"Would I be terribly rude if I didn't ask you to stay?" She laid her purse and keys on a marble-topped oak table.

"Aren't you feeling well, my dear?" He took her hand and brought it to his lips.

"I'm just a bit tired." She slowly eased her hand out of his. "Settling all of Tyler's affairs has been difficult for me."

"I understand. Everyone does." Glenn straightened his shoulders and looked directly at Lydia. "The people of Riverton think so highly of you."

"Are you trying to tell me something?"

"Oh, my dear, I hate to bring up the subject again, but it's that Cameron man."

Sighing deeply, Lydia shut her eyes, then quickly reopened them. "I've told you that Wade Cameron is a nice man who has stopped by a few times to check on me. I've become quite fond of his daughter."

"He knows you have friends who are looking out for you."

"But none of those friends understand what I'm going through the way Wa... Mr. Cameron does."

"Lydia, people are talking," Glenn said.

"So you and Eloise have told me."

"My dear, it would be foolish to risk your reputation over a man like that." The tone of Glenn's voice revealed his agitation.

"Just what is it that people think I'm doing with Mr. Cameron?"

Glenn gasped and shook his head. "Oh, my, no. Of course no one thinks that...that you'd have any sort of...intimate relationship with Cameron. However, his stopping by on a regular basis looks bad."

"Yes, I suppose it does."

"You really should explain the situation to him before he tries to insinuate himself further into your life."

"Thank you for your concern, Glenn." Lydia escorted her neighbor out onto the porch. "I really am quite tired, so if you don't mind—"

"Of course, of course." Glenn backed his way off the porch and down the steps. Standing on the sidewalk, he waved goodbye. "Don't forget I'm right next door if you need me."

Lydia forced a smile, waved pleasantly and slowly closed her front door. Taking a deep breath, she threw back her head and kicked her three-inch heels across the floor.

Mocha coffee, she thought. More than anything else, she wanted to curl up on the couch in the den with a cup of her favorite mocha coffee and a good old movie. A John Wayne Western would be nice.

She raced to her bedroom and slipped out of her suit. Looking around the lacy, feminine room, she decided it was a blessing that she and Tyler had kept separate bedrooms for nearly eight months before his death. What few memories she had of him in this room were faded by time. Hurriedly, she dressed in comfortable mustard slacks and matching sweater.

By the time she'd curled up on the couch with her second cup of coffee and found a good movie on television, the late-afternoon sun was flickering through the trees in the backyard and casting a shadowy glow over the den.

So seldom during her four-year marriage to Tyler had they ever enjoyed a Sunday afternoon at home together. There were always important people to see, places to go, movers and shakers to impress. It was the kind of life Lydia's mother and stepfather enjoyed, and she had convinced herself that it was what she wanted, too.

During that first, romantic year of marriage, she'd been so infatuated with her handsome young husband that she'd eagerly submitted to his every whim. Even after the rosy hue disappeared and she'd had to accept that their love would never be a grand passion, she had played the part of the perfect society wife, and Tyler had thanked her by taking lovers. She had suspected the truth all along, but hadn't had the courage to admit the possibility. She'd preferred to continue pretending that they had a normal marriage. But for months before the accident, even the promise of becoming the governor's wife hadn't eased the desperate depression she'd begun to feel.

Finishing the last delicious drop of coffee, Lydia savored the taste of chocolate still on her tongue. She set the cup down on the end table and focused her attention on the television screen. She'd found a John Wayne movie, but not a Western. The movie was one of her all-time favorites, but it was a love story, and she'd had second thoughts about watching it.

As John Wayne and Maureen O'Hara filled the screen with their magic presences, Lydia's heart swelled with the excitement she always felt when she watched this particular scene in *The Quiet Man*. With an Irish wind blowing her shimmering red hair, Maureen O'Hara succumbed to John Wayne's passionate embrace, and for one earth-shattering moment, Lydia Reid felt what the heroine felt. She closed her eyes and held the ecstasy within. She could feel strong arms around her, demanding lips covering hers and she knew that Wade Cameron was going to make love to her.

Lydia's eyes flew open. Her heart raced wildly. She buried her face in her hands and cried out, "No!" How could she be thinking of Wade Cameron with her husband dead only a few months? She had tried to convince herself that she felt nothing more than sympathy and understanding for Wade, that their acquaintance was simply something they both needed, temporarily, until the shock of what had happened to their respective mates wore off.

But she couldn't deny the intense desire she felt every time she thought of Wade, and she thought of him often. She had dreamed of him more than once, and in those dreams she'd discovered all the passion that had been lacking in her marriage.

These feelings were wrong and she knew it, but she couldn't stop them. Perhaps Glenn was right. She should explain to Wade how easily their innocent relationship could be misunderstood. After all, she had a reputation to uphold, and so did he if he cared at all about bringing up his daughter properly.

And if they kept seeing each other, she wasn't sure how long their relationship would remain innocent. She valued Wade's friendship. He'd become so important in her life—far too important.

Lydia checked her watch and wondered what Wade did at four o'clock on a Sunday afternoon. Perhaps she should phone and ask him to come over. If only she'd had the courage to say what needed to be said when he and Molly had stopped by yesterday. For the past six Saturdays she had gradually gotten to know and like the big, rugged farmer, and had grown to love his little girl. Of course, Wade really wasn't a farmer any longer. He had explained that a small-time farmer couldn't make a living these days, so he had invested more and more in cattle. There was money in beef, but he didn't have enough land to raise cattle on a large scale, so he'd also added two chicken houses for which he and his younger brother shared responsibilities.

There was such a quiet strength in Wade. Lydia enjoyed watching him talk and walk and loved listening to the sound of his deep, mellow voice. She knew his father had died when he'd been sixteen, and, as the eldest child, he had taken over and kept the farm going while helping his mother raise his younger brother and two sisters.

He never discussed his marriage to Macie other than to say it had ended years ago. And he never mentioned any other women.

The shrill ring of the telephone jarred Lydia from her thoughts. She got up, walked over to the desk and picked up the receiver. "Hello."

Silence.

"Hello," she said again.

"Stay away from Wade Cameron or you'll be sorry," the whispering voice said.

"What?" Lydia's hands quivered ever so slightly.

The dial tone sang out, ending the chilling phone message. She stood there with the receiver in her hand, staring down at the object as if it were some vile creature.

Oh, God! Who was this persistent caller? And why was he harassing her? The voice had been indistinguishable. Low, soft, raspy. It could have been male or female. Glenn had warned her. Eloise had warned her. Her own heart had warned her. And once again some stranger was issuing his or her own warning. Over the past few weeks, Lydia had received several calls from concerned friends and acquaintances advising her of how inappropriate her friendship with Wade Cameron was. And three other times a call had come from the mysterious stranger, but this was the first time the caller had actually threatened her.

With trembling fingers she picked up the telephone directory and found Wade's number. She dialed and waited, hoping he would be the one to answer.

"Hello," a tiny voice said.

For a split second she thought of hanging up, but didn't. "Hello, Molly. This is Lydia. May I speak to your father, please?"

"Yeah, just a minute. We're watching the football game." There was a moment of silence, then Lydia heard the child scream. "Daddy, it's for you."

The minutes ticked by while she waited. She'd begun to wonder if Molly Cameron had not gained her father's attention and had simply gone on her merry way, forgetting the phone call.

"Yeah." His voice sounded aggravated.

"This is Lydia Reid. I hope I haven't called at an inconvenient time."

"Lydia?"

"I'm sorry to bother you, but... but I was wondering if you could find time to stop by the house tonight." She didn't want to do this, but she knew she had no choice. She had to end this *thing* between them before it went any farther. She didn't trust herself to say no when Wade got around to asking for more than friendship, and she knew it was just a matter of time until that happened. In every look, smile, word and touch they exchanged was a sexual intensity that could only be harnessed for so long. Sooner or later it would break free and destroy them both.

"Is something wrong?"

"Not exactly. I just need to see you, to talk to you as soon as possible."

"An hour be all right?"

"Yes. Thank you."

Wade stood outside Lydia's back door, hesitating, knowing on some instinctive level that she had called him here to say goodbye. He'd been a fool to keep coming around. Sooner or later it was bound to cause trouble for her. The good people of Riverton weren't about to let their former first lady get involved with Wade Cameron, that country roughneck whose wife had scandalized the whole county with her whoring ways.

He wasn't too sure what kept him coming back week after week. Hormones, he guessed. Male sex drive. He had to admit that he wanted Lydia Reid so bad he lay awake at night hurting. What was it about her, he wondered, that made him crazy?

Without warning the sliding glass doors opened. Wade looked up right into Lydia's bright hazel eyes. Leo yipped several times. With his tongue and tail wagging in unison, the little mutt jumped up and down.

"I thought I heard your truck," she said. "Please, come on in."

He stepped inside the den, then unzipped his leather jacket. A gentle warmth surrounded him, the smell of wood burning in the fireplace permeating the air. Leo circled Wade, then began to sniff his boots.

"May I take your jacket?" she asked, accepting the brown leather coat when he removed it and handed it to her. "Leo, behave yourself."

"You said we needed to talk as soon as possible." Wade didn't want to waste any time with pleasantries. If she was kicking him out of her life, he wanted it done quickly and cleanly. No frills and fancy talk.

After hanging his jacket on a pine hall tree, she motioned for him to take a seat on the couch. "Sit down and I'll fix us some coffee." Leo followed every step Lydia made, his big brown eyes watching her adoringly.

"No coffee," he said abruptly.

"All right." She sat down on the couch and patted the cushion next to her, issuing him an invitation to join her. Leo lay down at her feet.

Wade couldn't look at her. He didn't want to see the pity in her eyes, that I'm-so-sorry-we-can't-be-friends look. "Just say what you've got to say."

"Please, Wade, sit down." Why wouldn't he look at her? she wondered. Did he already know what she was going to tell him? Had the gossip reached him, too?

Reluctantly he sat down, but kept his distance from her. The last thing he needed was to touch her. If he did, he wasn't sure he'd be able to let her go. "I can't stay long."

"You don't know how much your visits have meant to me. How much I've looked forward to seeing you and Molly every Saturday." She didn't want to do this. But she had no choice. It was better this way, for both of them. "No one else could possibly understand what I've gone through."

Wade jumped up, shoved his fists into his jeans pockets and turned his back to her. "Look, if you're trying, in your own ladylike way, to tell me to quit coming around, I understand. Don't waste your breath sugar-coating it, okay?"

Lydia stood, her knees weak, her hands trembling. Hearing the hurt and anger in his voice ripped her heart apart. Didn't he know how difficult this was for her? In some peculiar way, she needed him in her life. He was the one and only ray of sunshine in her dismal world. "Wade, please . . . let me explain."

"What's to explain?" He grabbed his coat, slipped it on and walked toward the door. "People are talking about us. Speculating about what's going on."

"I'm afraid that Tyler and Macie were the talk of the town, and now you and I are." Lydia wanted to reach out and touch his stiff back, to run a soothing hand over his tense shoulders. But she knew she shouldn't touch him. If she did . . .

"Yeah, and a lady like you doesn't want folks thinking she might be fooling around with some farm boy who raises chickens and cattle. Some guy with calluses on his hands and dirt under his fingernails." He slid open the door.

"We both have reputations, and I'm sure, for Molly's sake, you'd like yours to remain intact." Lydia followed him to the door, wishing she could make him understand that she hated saying goodbye. Leo followed, slipping beside Wade to run outside.

Wade turned around. The look on his face frightened Lydia. His eyes glowed like black fire and his lips curled into a snarl. "Lady, the only reputation I've ever had is bad. I was that wild Cameron kid when I was younger. You know, the boy who drank too much, drove too fast and laid anything female. Then one of those females caught me and I married her. I actually thought I was doing the honorable thing."

She held up her hand. It hovered mere inches from his face. She wanted to touch him, to ease his pain, but her hand froze in midair. "You don't have to—"

"You think it was rough finding out that your husband had been unfaithful the last couple of years? Well, lady, you don't know anything about being the object of people's pity and the brunt of other men's jokes."

"Oh, Wade." She dropped her hand. Tears began to form in her eyes, and their presence startled her. In the six months since Tyler's death, she hadn't been able to cry.

"If you slept with your husband after he started messing with Macie, you might want to get a checkup. Just in case. You see, my wife spread her legs for any man who wanted her."

The extent of Wade Cameron's misery washed over Lydia, and her own pain vanished. She wanted to take him in her arms and hold him, to comfort him and tell him how much she cared. And she did care, no matter how hard she'd tried not to. "Please don't leave."

"There's no point in my staying, is there?" He stepped outside onto the patio. A cool October wind tousled his hair. He ran his hand through the curls trying to undo the damage.

She wanted to beg him not to leave. This wasn't the way she'd imagined things would end. If only he weren't in so much pain, he might be able to accept the fact that there was no future for them, that their being together would only bring them both more misery.

He looked so lonely standing there with the dark, moonlit sky at his back. He looked as lonely as she felt. "I received a threatening phone call right before I telephoned you."

"You what?" He glared at her, disbelief in his black eyes.

Stepping outside, she instantly felt the chilly night air engulf her. "Someone, I don't have any idea who, called and warned me to stay away from you."

His gaze narrowed, taking in the uncertainty in her eyes. "You got a threatening phone call?"

"It wasn't the only call I've received."

What the hell was going on here? he wondered. Was she trying to tell him that she was ending their friendship because some mysterious caller had threatened her? "How many times has this person called you?"

"They've called four times, but until tonight I thought the calls were like the ones I'd received from other people. I thought it was someone calling simply out of concern. But now I'm not so certain. Tonight this person actually threatened me." She looked at Wade, relieved that she'd shared her secret with him. "Who would do something like that?"

"Well, you might question our new mayor and see if he knows anything about it." Wade knew that Glenn Haraway had more reason to want to keep Lydia away from another man than anyone else in town. And considering Haraway's reputation for manipulating the law for his own purposes, Wade didn't think he was above trying to frighten Lydia.

"Glenn?"

"Yeah, Glenn," Wade said. "Just in case you haven't figured it out, Haraway has the hots for you."

"That isn't true." Lydia clutched her arms, running her hands up and down in an effort to warm herself.

"Could be he's afraid I'll get in your bed before he does."

Lydia gasped. "How dare you say such a thing!"

"Well, I can't think of anyone else who'd have a reason, can you?"

"What about you? Isn't there someone in your life who might not want us together?"

Instantly his mother came to mind, but he brushed aside the notion. Ruthie Cameron wasn't the type to make threatening phone calls. If she had a bone to pick with someone, she met them head-on in a face-to-face confrontation. "No one in my life would have any reason to feel threatened by you."

Wade hated the idea that someone had frightened Lydia, even more than he rebelled at the thought that the whole town had been advising her to stay away from him. He'd like nothing better than to get his hands on the mysterious caller, but he doubted that Lydia would want him involved, especially if his suspicions about Haraway turned out to be true. "I think you should notify the police," Wade said.

"I'd rather not, unless the situation worsens." She saw the questioning look in Wade's eyes. "If I call the police, there will be even more gossip. Something like this wouldn't stay a secret for long."

"Yeah, you're right." Hell! What else could he say to her? If she was more worried about town gossip than she was in apprehending the mystery caller, then there was no way he could help her. Besides, if they ended their relationship, there would be no reason for any more phone calls, either giving advice or issuing warnings.

"You do understand, don't you?" she asked, wondering if a man like Wade could ever truly appreciate the delicate balance she had to maintain in her life. She had been taught since childhood that appearances were of the utmost importance.

He turned to go. "Sure I understand. For you, being the talk of the town is a fate worse than death."

"I don't want you to leave like this," she said.

"How?"

"Angry."

"Oh, so you don't want me to leave angry, huh? How do you want me to leave?"

She almost said she didn't want him to leave at all, that she wanted him to stay so they could talk and laugh and enjoy each other's company. "I'd like for us to part on friendly terms."

"I thought you'd finally figured it out," he said, taking a tentative step toward her.

"Figured what out?"

"You and I can't be just friends."

She felt the blood rush to her face and an inner warmth spread through her body. Their eyes met in a clash of instant understanding. He wanted her. She wanted him. Their need was elemental.

"I can't offer you more," she said, all the while wishing she could give him everything he wanted. It would be so easy to clasp his hand and lead him back inside. He would take her in his arms and kiss her. He would roam his hands over her body and slowly remove her clothes. He would pick her up and carry her to bed. He would stand over her, looking down with wild desire while he stripped away his jeans and shirt. And then he would come to her, fill her, and...

Wade recognized the longing in her eyes and knew she wanted him as much as he wanted her. He wondered what she'd do if he pushed her back inside and kissed the breath out of her. "I don't want to be just your friend. We've tried that and it just hasn't worked, has it? I want to be your lover and you know it."

"We can't." She realized she was going to lose him, and there was nothing she could do about it.

"See you around then." Hell, he didn't want to leave her, but he wasn't about to beg Lydia to let him stay. He'd made a fool of himself over a woman once, and her betrayal had almost destroyed him.

Lydia reached out and took hold of his hand just as he started to walk away. "Wade." She knew touching him would be a mistake, but she couldn't stop herself.

The feel of her slender fingers wrapped over his hard knuckles sent a gut-wrenching jolt through him. He stopped, but didn't turn around. Her hand trembled. "You'd better go in. It's getting pretty cool out here." His voice softened, the tone one of concern.

She clung to his hand, the very feel of him a sensual pleasure. "Take care of yourself."

"Yeah, you too."

Standing in the darkness, he took one last look. Her body, silhouetted by the den lights, was pure temptation. If he didn't get the hell away from her right now, he was going to pick her up, carry her inside and make love to her.

He pulled away. Her hand fell free. With a swift, steady stride, he walked to his truck, got inside and started the engine. Shivering from the cool wind, Lydia watched as he backed out of the driveway. She ran to the edge of the yard and gazed down the street until she no longer saw the red dots from his taillights. Hot, salty tears streamed down her face. Wade Cameron was gone.

Five

"**I** won't do it," Lydia said, slamming the file folder down on Glenn Haraway's desk.

Glenn jumped up from his plush executive chair and, wringing his slender hands together, rushed over to the highly agitated woman glaring at him. "Please, lower your voice, my dear."

"Oh, I'm sorry. We wouldn't want your office staff to know that you've just asked me to prostitute myself so that your administration can take credit for acquiring a new Riverton mall." Lydia whirled around, picked up her taupe leather purse from the chair and walked to the door.

"No, no. I'm the one who's sorry." Glenn closed his fingers about her upper arm, momentarily halting her departure. "I never meant for my suggestion to upset you so. It's just that the council and I have done everything but get down on our knees and beg Mrs. Cameron to sell. She's determined to keep those old buildings intact. She says she can't bear to see them torn down. We simply thought that if you spoke to her son, she might—''

"A month ago you were warning me to stay away from Wade Cameron. You and Eloise and all our friends were so concerned about my reputation.'' Lydia stared at Glenn's hand where it gripped her arm. He released her immediately. "Now y'all want me to invite him to lunch and try to convince him to persuade his mother to sell the old gin and the land surrounding it.''

"I should think you'd want to see this project become a reality. After all, it was Tyler's baby. He's the one who went out and found the investors and the one who got releases from all the other land owners down there along Cotton Row. Time is running out, Lydia. Something has to be done.''

"Of course, I'd like to see Riverton get a modern shopping mall, but I don't like the idea of using my...my acquaintance with Wade in order to persuade his mother to sign a release.''

"You wouldn't have to ask him to your house. You could ask him to meet you at a restaurant, or even meet him here. Tell him when you call that it's about business." Glenn placed his arm around Lydia's shoulders and led her back into his office. "You know I'm the last person on earth who'd want to see you spending time with Wade Cameron." He ran the back of his hand down her cheek. "Or any other man, for that matter.''

Lydia took several quick, calming breaths. Although Glenn had been a perfect gentleman since Tyler's death, recently he'd made it perfectly clear that after an appropriate amount of time had passed, he intended to woo and win his best friend's widow.

She moved away from his caressing hand. "I doubt Mr. Cameron would meet with me considering we didn't part on the best of terms.''

"There's no way to know unless you call and ask." Glenn picked up his phone and handed it to her.

"I won't meet with him alone." She wondered if Glenn would suspect there was more to her reluctance than a distaste for being used.

"Ask him to meet you here. I'll sit in on the whole thing. Perfectly respectable. No way Cameron or anyone else can read more into it."

She hated the whole idea and knew that Glenn and the other council members were simply taking advantage of her brief friendship with Wade Cameron to reach a goal. Strange how well-mannered Southern gentlemen could bend the rules when it was necessary to get what they wanted. She told herself to forget the whole thing. She'd been used as a political tool by Tyler for four years, and she didn't have to do this sort of thing anymore. But her heart told her that she wanted to see Wade, and any excuse was better than none.

Five weeks without seeing him, without hearing his voice, without waiting eagerly for Saturday afternoons to arrive. It was as if she were in mourning for two different men at the same time, and the comparison made her wonder if she'd ever truly loved Tyler Reid. During the long, endless days, she often caught herself daydreaming about Wade, about something he'd said or the way his Adam's apple moved when he swallowed or how his brown eyes were so dark they looked black. And she missed Molly, that bright bundle of energy whose very presence had turned her immaculately decorated house into a home.

At night she dreamed of Wade and would awaken hot and damp and wanting. She'd never known what it was like to want a man so desperately. It was lust, animalistic lust, and she felt ashamed to admit that she, Lydia Lee Milner Reid, was capable of such wanton desire.

"Well?" Glenn asked, still holding the phone out to her. "Riverton needs that mall. Do it for me."

She stared at the phone, conflicting emotions raging inside her. "I'm not sure."

"Do it for Tyler. Consider it one last duty as his wife."

Lydia grabbed the phone and dialed Wade's number, never once asking herself why she had it memorized.

Wade hung his cap and denim jacket on a metal wall rack just inside the screened back porch. Kicking the mud from his work boots, he took a whiff of his mother's chicken stew. Peering inside, he saw his mother setting the table. He wiped his feet on the braided rug lying in front of the door before walking into the warm, old-fashioned kitchen.

"Something sure smells good," Wade said. "What's that cooking besides stew?"

"Peach cobbler," Ruthie replied as she turned her black eyes on her elder son. "No hurry about washing up. Britt and Tanya are coming for supper, so it'll be another hour."

"I'm starving and you tell me I've got to wait on my baby brother and his always-late wife? Have they patched up their differences or will we have to sit through another meal with the two of them not speaking?"

"You can bring in some more wood for the fireplace and fill up the heater with kerosene." Ruthie opened the oven door and removed a huge cast iron skillet filled with crackling grease. "That ought to give you enough to do while we're waiting."

"You always could find more chores for a man to do."

"I'm trying to stay out of Britt and Tanya's business, but I'm worried. Maybe you should talk to your brother, see if there's any way we can help."

"I'll think about it." Wade picked up his clean mug from the counter and poured himself a cup of piping hot coffee. "What's Molly doing?"

"Homework." Ruthie poured corn bread batter into the skillet, slipped the skillet back in the hot oven, and closed the door.

"Homework in the first grade?"

"It's an art assignment. They're doing some sort of Christmas book." Ruthie shook her head and grunted.

"They're having a Christmas party and all the mamas are invited. She wanted to know if I'd come."

"What'd you tell her?"

"I told her that her grandma was too old for such stuff." Shaking her head again, Ruthie looked down at her work-worn hands. "As much as I want to do right by that child, I know if I go to her school party, I'd wind up embarrassing her. And that'd break both our hearts."

"Ma, you don't have to explain to me. I know how much you love Molly."

"I wouldn't fit in with all those young, bright mamas, an old war horse like me. I'd be bound to say or do the wrong thing and shame Molly."

"Damn, I wish I could take off work and go."

"Britt would cover for you here." Ruthie smiled and swatted away a tear that had escaped from the corner of her eye. "That child needs a mama of her own. Some young gal who knows about school parties and such."

"Hell, I'll go." Wade pulled out a chair and sat down at the kitchen table. "I'll probably be the only rooster in the henhouse, but Molly's had to do without too much. Macie never could be bothered to go to any of Molly's parties at play school or kindergarten."

Wade finished off his coffee in silence while his mother busily continued preparing supper. When he got up to go back outside for the firewood, Ruthie placed her hand on his arm.

"Lydia Reid called."

"Lydia called here?"

"Said she needed to talk to you."

Wade felt his insides warming at the thought of the beautiful woman who had plagued his nights and haunted his days. "She wants me to call her back?"

"Said anytime tonight."

Wade turned toward the hall where the only phone in the house adorned the top of a rickety pine table near the staircase.

"She said it was business," Ruthie called out.

He picked up the phone, dialed her number and waited, like a green kid with his first girlfriend. The moment he heard her voice, his body tightened with arousal.

"Yeah, it's Wade Cameron. I'm returning your call."

Wade got out of his truck, slammed the door and stepped up on the sidewalk in front of Stanley's Steak House. The November sun touched his cheeks with its warmth, but the cool wind reminded him that winter was near. He walked into the restaurant and waited for the hostess. The place was crowded for a late-Saturday afternoon. Noticing several customers looking his way, Wade felt uneasy and wondered if they were watching to see who he was meeting.

The hostess greeted him with a smile. When he told her he was meeting Mrs. Reid, the young woman's smile widened. He unzipped his leather jacket and straightened the collar of his plaid shirt.

Then he saw her. She was sitting at a booth beside the windows. The sunlight turned her light brown hair to dark gold. She was wearing a pink wool dress the exact shade of her soft, pink lips. A single strand of pearls circled her neck and rested on the rise of her breasts. Matching pearl studs graced her ears where wisps of her fine hair curled away from the neat chignon.

Even though he hadn't seen her in weeks, she'd never been out of his thoughts, and the image of her beautiful face was one he carried with him day and night. It had taken every ounce of his willpower to stay away from her. And now here he was invited to lunch. He couldn't imagine what *business* the two of them had to discuss. He figured she'd made up some excuse to see him because she'd missed him as much as he'd missed her.

Lydia looked up just as the waitress moved aside to allow Wade access to the booth. Warmth flooded through her like summer sunshine on naked flesh. Her stomach quivered. Her heart fluttered. She felt totally foolish. A member of the opposite sex hadn't made her this nervous since she'd been thirteen and madly in love with one of her older brother's friends. Funny, she couldn't remember the boy's name, but she did remember that he'd looked at Bill Milner's skinny, flat-chested little sister as if she weren't even there.

Her feelings for that long-forgotten boy had been innocent, but there was absolutely nothing innocent about the emotions Wade Cameron stirred to life within her. She knew how utterly wrong those feelings were, but she simply wasn't able to restrain them. For the first time in her life, Lydia Reid felt out of control.

She watched him move toward her, stop and smile. His smile melted her heart. There was so much warmth and friendliness in his dark eyes, such happiness in his expression. He was devastating. Tall, dark, rugged and the most masculine male she'd ever known. There was such a gentle strength about him, as if he was aware of the power contained in his big body and deliberately kept it in check.

He wore a red and blue plaid flannel shirt beneath his leather jacket and a pair of standard denim jeans covered his lean hips and his long powerful thighs. His brown boots gleamed with the patina of fine old leather.

Lydia forced herself to extend her hand. Wade hesitated momentarily, then took her hand in his. "Thank you for coming," she said. "Please sit down."

Reluctantly he released her hand and slid into the booth so that he sat opposite her. "I'm glad you invited me." He noticed the hostess hadn't left. He looked up at her questioningly.

"Oh," the young woman gasped as if caught doing something naughty. "Your waitress will be here in just a minute." She handed Wade a menu, then laid one down in front of Lydia. "Can I get you folks a drink?"

"Coffee," Lydia said, but didn't take her eyes off Wade. Although his image had never left her thoughts, seeing the real man made her realize how inadequate the fantasy was.

"Make that two." He didn't turn his attention to Lydia until the hostess departed. "I've missed you," he whispered.

Oh, Lord, how did she reply? Did she dare tell him the truth? No, she couldn't. This was a business luncheon and nothing more, she reminded herself. Could he possibly think her phone call had been personal? "I've missed our talks, Wade. I think we were good for each other, and we needed each other in order to get through some difficult times after Tyler and Macie were killed."

The smile faded from his face. His jaw tightened and the pulse at his temple jerked several times. "I take it you've been doing okay? No more threatening phone calls?"

"No, not since the last time I saw you. They called about thirty minutes after you left and warned me to stay away from you. Nothing since then."

The waitress appeared and placed glasses of water and linen-wrapped silverware in front of them. "You folks ready to order?"

"We need a few more minutes." Wade's voice sounded gruff, and he wasn't surprised when the blond waitress stared at him with wide eyes and scurried away.

"I think you scared her to death." Lydia straightened her back against the plush leather booth as she casually gazed around the restaurant to see if anyone had taken note of her and her luncheon companion.

"You got another phone call after I left that night?" he asked, leaning over the table, reaching out for her hand that rested on top of the menu. "Could you tell if it was a man or a woman?"

"No, the voice sounded muffled and raspy, the way it always does." She pulled her hand away before he could touch her.

"Did you call the police?"

"No."

"Then you should have at least let me know."

"We'd just agreed not to see each other again. Besides, it was the last call I received."

"Same person?" he asked.

"Yes."

"What did they say?"

"Whoever it was simply warned me not to keep on seeing you or...or I'd be sorry." She glanced at him, her heart hammering loudly, her stomach quivering.

"Damn!"

"Lower your voice. People are staring at us."

He felt as if she'd slapped him. Ever the lady concerned about appearances. He wished Macie had had half Lydia's respect for propriety, but he wished Lydia had a bit less. "Why did you ask me to meet you for lunch?"

"Why don't we order first." Lydia picked up the menu, opened it and scanned the pages. "Business can wait till later."

"All right." He followed her lead by picking up his menu. Business? What business could they possibly have to discuss?

It was obvious to Lydia that Wade Cameron hadn't come here to talk business. He had been under the mistaken impression that their meeting was personal and seemed upset that it wasn't. She wished she could tell him what she was feeling: that more than anything she wanted to be with him, talk to him, share his most intimate thoughts. But she didn't dare allow herself the pleasure of his company. If she didn't stay away from him, she'd be lost. Although she considered herself a strong woman, she didn't think she had the strength to resist the look of desire she saw in Wade's eyes.

Their lunch seemed to take forever, both of them eating quietly, occasionally exchanging idle chitchat. She told him she had gone to Alabama and spent Thanksgiving with her brother's family. They talked about his chicken houses and his cattle, about the long hours he spent trying to keep his family business solvent, about her tentative plans to return to interior design and how she had decided to give most of her inheritance from Tyler to charity.

"I don't need Tyler's money," she said. "Considering what a sham our marriage was, I'd feel guilty if I kept it."

"I'd say he owed it to you for everything he put you through." Wade laid his fork on his plate and pushed it away.

"I'd much rather take care of myself. If everything works out the way I'm hoping it will, I can rent one of the spaces in the new mall for my interior design firm."

"What new mall?" Wade eyed her suspiciously.

"You know about the plans to tear down all those old buildings along Cotton Row and put up a beautiful, modern shopping mall." Lydia's heart raced ninety miles an hour, and moisture coated the palms of her hands.

"I thought since several of the land owners wouldn't sell, the investors were looking for other acreage." Wade knew that his mother, Horace Pounders and Marcus Holt had refused to sell their property.

"There isn't a more ideal location in all of Riverton." Lydia wiped her hands on her napkin and laid it on the table. "I can't imagine why anyone would want to hang on to land down there on Cotton Row. Goodness, there's nothing but a bunch of dilapidated old buildings and those rusted railroad tracks."

"I take it that you're in favor of tearing down part of Riverton's history to make way for progress."

"You say that as if you think I have no regard for preserving our heritage, and that just isn't so." She clutched the edge of the table with her hands and glared at the big, dark man sitting across from her. How dare he accuse her of disrespect for Southern heritage. "I happen to belong to the Historical Society, and I've worked diligently to help preserve many of the pre-Civil War structures in Riverton."

"Then why not save Cotton Row?" he asked and nodded a thanks to the waitress as she refilled his coffee cup.

"Ma will never sell that land if it means the old gin and the other buildings will be torn down."

Lydia released her tenacious hold on the table and tried to relax. Watching the waitress pour more coffee into her cup, Lydia warned herself to calm down unless she wanted to lose her temper and risk acting in an unladylike manner. "It would cost more to preserve those old buildings than it would to build a new mall."

"So?"

"Statistics show that people want something new and modern in Riverton, in most Southern towns." When she saw the stern look of disapproval on Wade's face, she took a deep breath. "If your mother sold her property, it would help you and your brother repay the bank loan you took out to buy those new chicken houses."

"If my mother decided to sell her land, the money would be hers. Besides, there are other owners not willing to sell."

Lydia shook her head. "Your mother is the only one who hasn't agreed to sign a release."

"What about old man Pounders and Marcus Holt?"

"Glenn has been able to persuade Mr. Pounders to sign a release, and he tells me that Mr. Holt is on the verge of changing his mind."

"I see."

"I'm not asking for Glenn, or even for Tyler. I'm asking for the town. Riverton needs to move forward. This little town has remained in the past for far too long."

"You're talking to the wrong Cameron," Wade said. "The land where the old cotton gin is located belongs to my mother. It was her only inheritance from her father."

"I realize your mother holds the deed to the land, but I thought if you could talk to her, explain the benefits for herself and her family as well as the entire town of Riverton . . . well, we . . . er . . . I thought if anyone could make her see reason, it would be you."

Wade balled his hand into a fist and slammed it down on the table. The entire booth shook from the force of his blow.

Lydia's eyes widened in horror. People at nearby tables turned to stare.

"Well, you thought wrong, lady." He stood up, his dark eyes blazing with contempt at the woman whose beautiful face had turned deathly pale and whose eyes expressed her shock.

"Wade." Although his anger frightened her, the fear was not for her physical safety. It broke her heart to know how badly she'd hurt him. Oh, God, she hadn't meant for him to react like this, as if she had betrayed him.

He glowered at her for a brief moment, then reached in his pocket for his wallet. He threw down several crisp green bills and walked away, his long legs moving with great speed. Lydia sat immobile while whispering voices and curious stares bombarded her from every side. Without a thought of how her actions might be assessed, she got up and followed Wade. By the time she caught up with him, he was getting into his truck.

"Wade, please wait." With her hands clasped together in an almost pleading gesture, Lydia stood in front of the mud-spattered blue truck.

He stopped dead still and turned to face her. Without saying a word, he told her how he felt. It was there in his eyes, in the way he frowned and the way his chest rose and fell with his labored breathing.

"Please, let me explain." She took a tentative step in his direction.

"What's there to explain? You and Haraway and God knows who else thought you could use me, use the way I feel about you, to get what you wanted."

"It wasn't like that." She cringed when she heard him groan in disgust. "I truly believe the new mall is important to Riverton."

"You know what you can do with your new mall, Mrs. Reid." He stepped up into the truck and slammed the door.

She'd made a terrible mistake, and she was so sorry. If only she could change what had happened, if only there was some way to make him forgive her. "Wade!"

She didn't care that people on the busy Riverton street were staring at her, that more than one shop owner was peering out their windows to see the elegant Lydia Reid screeching at Wade Cameron like a fishwife.

Irrational with the need to soothe his pain, Lydia grabbed hold of the passenger door and swung it open just as Wade shoved the truck into reverse. While he turned to check his rearview mirror, Lydia jumped into the cab of the truck and pulled the door closed with a bang.

"What the hell?" He turned to find her sitting beside him, her straight skirt hiked several inches above her knees, a wide run in her stockings and deep scuffs scarring the side of one pink leather shoe.

"I'm not through talking to you," she said breathlessly.

"What do you mean, jumping in the truck that way?"

"You wouldn't wait."

"Get out."

"No." She smoothed the perspiration from her upper lip with her fingertips. She'd risked serious injury by leaping into his truck just as he started to back out of the parking place, and the realization of what she'd done suddenly struck her as funny.

When she began laughing, he stared at her as if she'd lost her mind. "What the hell are you laughing about?"

She couldn't seem to stop giggling, the insanity of the situation making her light-headed.

"Mrs. Reid, are you aware that half the people in town are watching us?" Wade asked, wondering how long it would take her to regret her foolish actions.

"Then take me out of town," she said, the remnants of a smile still on her lips.

He glared at her, his gaze questioning her statement, searching her face for a denial. He saw none. Quickly he backed up the truck and headed east. Neither of them spoke as they drove out of Riverton.

Five minutes later Wade drove over the deserted railroad tracks that led to Cotton Row, two city blocks of crumbling concrete, broken windows, rotting lumber and empty, weed-infested lots. He maneuvered the Ford into the drive beside the old cotton gin which stood tall and wide like the carcass of an ancient mammoth, it too belonging to a time long since passed.

Wade put the keys in his pocket, opened the door and got out. Lydia waited for him to circle the truck and help her down. When he walked in the opposite direction, she sat and watched him. The wind blew dead leaves and bits of decaying trash across the dirt drive and swept Wade's dark curls down onto his forehead. With one big hand, he brushed the strands out of his eyes.

Lydia opened her door and stepped down, almost losing her balance. She wasn't accustomed to trucks. She'd never ridden in one before today.

With slow, unsteady steps she followed him across the empty lot next to the old gin. When she was within a few feet of him, he turned.

"Well?" His voice held nothing but contempt for her.

"Well what?" she snapped.

"You said you weren't through talking and asked me to take you out of town." He shoved his hands into the pockets of his jacket and kicked at the loose gravel beneath his feet.

"Glenn did ask me to speak to you about the mall," she said. When Wade didn't respond in any way, she continued, "At first I said no. You and I had agreed not to see each other again, and... well, we didn't exactly say good-bye as friends."

"But Haraway persuaded you to try to use me, anyway." Wade turned his back on her.

"The truth is..." Did she have the courage to be honest with him? she wondered. "The truth is, I've missed you, and I agreed to this meeting because I so desperately wanted to see you.''

His whole body stiffened as if he'd been dipped in cement. He looked like some huge, dark statue silhouetted against a crisp blue sky and a slowly setting sun.

She placed her hand on his back and the statue crumbled with one giant breath. He turned, jerked her into his arms and held her to him with a passionate possessiveness that shook her to the very core of her being.

"Lydia," he breathed the word against her neck, his lips brushing her naked skin.

"Please don't hate me." She slipped her arms around his waist and squeezed with all her might.

He raised his head and looked down at her. She was so much shorter and smaller than he. Such a delicate woman. "Hate is the last thing I feel for you."

When she sighed with relief, he took the opportunity to cover her open mouth with his own, his tongue plunging into the welcoming warmth. Although startled by his sudden possession, her body accepted him as if it had been waiting a lifetime to know such pure pleasure.

His lips claimed hers with repeated thoroughness as his hands stroked her from neck to hips. Wild with his need for her, Wade trembled, his breath coming hard and fast. He felt her softening, becoming pliant and giving beneath his touch.

She had never felt like this, and the very intensity of her passion frightened her. Her response was as uninhibited as his demands, and Lydia knew that she had to escape before she reached the point of no return.

Standing in the shadows of yesterday, lost in the rapture of Wade's embrace, Lydia learned the meaning of desire. It was as strong and powerful as the wind, yet as sweet and untainted as the sunset. Here in Wade Cameron's arms she could feel a special bond growing between them, one she feared could never be severed.

"Oh, lady, lady, do you have any idea how much I want you?" He showered her face with tiny kisses while his hands roamed down her hips, cupping her bottom and crushing her against his arousal.

"Don't do this to me," she said, trying to pull away from him, her body yearning for more while her mind warned her that she was playing with fire.

"I'm not doing anything to you that you aren't doing to me." Still clasping her bottom, he rubbed her against him. "You want this. I know you do."

She laid her head on his chest and listened to the sound of his accelerated heartbeat. "I can't deny how I feel, but I can and must deny us both what we want."

"No." He stepped away from her, letting his hands fall free. "You don't mean that."

"We can't act on these feelings. It would be wrong." She had to make him understand that she wasn't the kind of woman who could make love without a commitment, without loving and being loved.

"It would be wrong if we don't. Can't you see that?"

"I never should have met you today. I'm sorry."

He grabbed her face in his big hands, searching her clear hazel eyes for the answer he wanted. It wasn't there. Desire as hot and consuming as what he felt shone in their golden green depths, but restraint held that longing in check. "It's not going to stop until we have each other, you know that, don't you?"

"This has to be goodbye," she said, choking back the tears lodged in her throat. "Otherwise we're going to destroy each other."

He wanted to argue with her, to tell her that they couldn't fight this overwhelming attraction they felt, but he knew his words would be useless. She was a lady, a widow in mourning, and there was no way he could force her to forget her moral upbringing, her regard for propriety and her personal sense of right and wrong. Those were all qualities he admired, part of the reason he was so attracted to her. But right now he wished she were a little bit more woman and a little less lady.

Looking around at the emptiness on Cotton Row, he suddenly felt as lonely as the old buildings appeared to be. "I don't think Ma will ever sell this land. She's a woman who doesn't like change."

Lydia reached up and ran her fingers down his cheek. "If things were different, I think I'd like getting to know your mother."

He pulled her hand to his lips and kissed her open palm. "I'll take you home."

"Thank you."

The wind whistled eerily through the broken windows in the old gin, and mauve shadows fell across Lydia and Wade. Devouring each other with one last, hungry look, they tried to say goodbye to a passion they both knew would never die.

Six

Wade sat at the bar, his big hand draped around a warm mug that had, an hour ago, contained his second frosty beer. A live band played the latest country hit while New Year's revelers crowded the dance floor. It had been months since he'd stopped by Hooligan's, the state-line roadhouse famous for loud music, good liquor, bad women and an occasional fistfight. Wade had lost his taste for frequenting honky-tonks years ago, before Molly had been born. But tonight he'd felt alone, more alone than he'd felt in years.

Tanya had dragged Britt off to a late-night church service, and Molly had fallen asleep in her grandmother's lap before nine o'clock. Wade had rambled around the big old farmhouse, listening to the slowly falling rain hitting the metal roof on the back porch. Looking out into the dark, starless night, all Wade could see was Lydia Reid's face. For the past month he had tried, unsuccessfully, to put her out of his mind, but the harder he tried, the more he thought about her. And every time he thought about her, he got aroused.

By ten o'clock he'd been pacing the floor, sick with wanting, hot for a woman. He knew he could find one at Hooligans. For the past hour, he'd rebuffed more than one advance while he sat brooding and nursing his beer. One woman had been too old, another too skinny and another too tall. Right now, a bosomy redhead was giving him the eye. She wasn't a day over twenty-five, possessed a voluptuous yet petite figure, and was making it plain that she was available. Wearing skin-tight jeans, a silky, see-through shirt that revealed naked flesh and a pair of dark aureoles, the woman leaned against the bar, her small feet encased in a pair of four-inch heels.

He didn't want to admit that the reason he'd rejected those other three women was because he wanted Lydia Reid and no one else. Hell, she was just a woman like any other, with warm kissable lips, firm, hand-filling breasts and two legs just waiting to wrap themselves around a man. He could find the same thing with the redhead, he told himself, and pushed away from the bar.

Taking his time walking to the end of the bar where the willing woman stood, Wade wondered where Lydia Reid was tonight, who she was with and what she was doing.

The redhead smiled up at him when he stopped in front of her. "Hi, there," she said, her voice little-girl soft.

"Dance?" He nodded toward the crowd of partying couples wrapped in each other's arms.

"I thought you'd never ask."

Wade draped his arm around her shoulders. She cuddled up against him as he led her out onto the dance floor. Turning around, she went into his arms and settled herself against him intimately, her breasts crushed against his chest, her stomach pressing against his arousal.

"I like the way you feel, sugar." She rubbed against him, laying her head on his chest.

They moved around, dancing, hugging, her body stroking his to the rhythm of the guitars and drums. He was ready. She was willing. All he had to do was ask.

He hadn't had a woman in a long time. But he wanted one now. Unfortunately the one he wanted wasn't the one he held in his arms.

"Would you like to take me home?" the redhead asked, then bit gently on Wade's earlobe.

He reached down, grabbing her hip and shoving her against him. God, he needed a woman. Bad! But not this woman, not any woman except Lydia Reid.

"I'm flattered you'd ask," he said, knowing he'd led this woman on and owed her more than a hasty dismissal. "But I'd be using you to forget someone else. You wouldn't want that, would you?"

She looked up at him and smiled. "I've been used before."

"But not by me." He stopped dancing and led her back to the bar, turning to the bartender. "Hey, Snake, give the lady another drink, on me." Wade pulled out his wallet, removed several bills and laid them down, then leaned over to kiss his dance partner on the cheek.

When he started to walk away, the redhead grabbed his wrist. "Does she know how lucky she is?"

Wade laughed, a sound somewhere between a chuckle and grunt. Without answering, he retrieved his leather jacket, slipped into it and headed for the exit, looking forward to taking a deep breath of fresh air. The smell of smoke and liquor and human perspiration hung in the air, thick and heavy.

The moment he opened the door, he saw that the slow, steady rain had turned to sleet. Zipping up his brown bomber jacket, he pulled his keys out of his pocket and made a mad dash for his truck. He jumped inside the dark, cold cab, slamming the door and shaking the moisture from his body. With chilled fingers he raked through his damp hair and looked at the seat where his forgotten Stetson rested.

He put the keys in the ignition, started the truck and backed out of the parking lot. When he reached the highway, he turned toward town. He knew where he had to go, what he had to do. He just hoped she wouldn't send him away.

Lydia stood by the canopy bed, only the glow from a small table lamp illuminating the dark room. She'd been home from the country club New Year's dance less than thirty minutes, alone for less than half an hour and yet she felt suffocated by loneliness.

She'd taken off her blue chiffon evening gown, placed it back in its protective bag and hung it in the closet. After tossing her slip on a nearby chair, Lydia stripped down to her white lace bikini panties.

Even though the world outside was slowly turning into a winter wonderland, her home was warm and cosy, but empty—so very, very empty.

She really hadn't wanted to go to the dance, but Glenn and Eloise had insisted, telling her that *everyone* was expecting her to make an appearance. And they'd been right. Everyone had bombarded her with sympathetic questions about her life. Everyone had given her suggestions about how to cope with losing the man she'd loved, and they'd told her that time would mend her broken heart. Everyone female had made subtle little references to Wade Cameron, wondering, out of genuine concern, about her relationship with Macie's former husband. Everyone male had asked her to dance, then at least half of those males had, in a gentlemanly manner, propositioned her.

Lydia had never been so glad to see a night and a year end. She glanced over at the illuminated bedside clock. Twenty-five minutes after one. A brand new year.

Soon, she'd have to make some decisions. She couldn't go on aimlessly the way she'd been doing since Tyler's death in late April. She could leave Riverton, go back to Birmingham and reopen her interior design firm. It would take time, but she knew she could rebuild her business.

Yet somehow, she didn't think leaving would be the answer. In the five years since she'd moved to Mississippi as a bride, she'd grown to love the state and especially the small northeastern town she called home.

However, leaving would eliminate a rather serious problem she would have to face in a few months. Glenn Haraway had made it perfectly clear tonight that when Lydia's year of mourning ended, he intended to pursue a personal relationship with her. He'd even admitted that only his respect for her and his years of friendship with Tyler prevented him from asking her to marry him now.

Lydia didn't love Glenn, and she had no intention of marrying him. She had loved Tyler and their marriage had turned into a disaster. She had no intention of rushing into another lifelong commitment.

Of course, if she left town, she wouldn't be faced with the possibility of seeing Wade Cameron again. For over a month, she'd both dreaded and dreamed of the day that they would run into each other, but it hadn't happened. Knowing that she had no right to want a man so totally unsuitable for her, a man who, by his own admission, never intended to remarry, a man whose wife had been Tyler's lover, didn't stop her from thinking about him night and day. The man had become an obsession.

Ever since she'd made a fool of herself by jumping into his truck, the whole town had started gossiping again about the mayor's widow and Wade Cameron. There had been two more mysterious phone calls. One came the very night after she'd seen Wade for the last time. Two weeks later, right before Christmas, the second call came on a Sunday afternoon. The voice had told her she was being smart not to see that redneck farmer again.

Suddenly Lydia realized she was wringing her hands. She hadn't been this nervous since the last time she'd seen Wade and didn't understand what was wrong with her now.

You're lying to yourself, she said silently. You know exactly what's wrong with you. You're a normal, healthy, young woman. And you're in heat. You need a man. And you want Wade Cameron.

She looked down at her hands, clasped together in front of her and noticed that she was twisting around her wedding band and diamond ring. Without thinking, she slipped both off her finger, held them in the palm of her hand and stared at them. She should have taken them off months ago. They didn't mean anything to her anymore. They were simply reminders of four wasted years and of a man who had betrayed her—not once, but time and time again.

She opened the nightstand drawer, dropped the rings inside and closed the drawer. Reaching down to the foot of the bed, she picked up her ivory silk robe and put it on, belting it loosely.

Restlessly she moved about the room, wide awake and longing for a man she couldn't have. She'd been a virgin when she'd married Tyler, but not totally inexperienced. She had loved her husband and longed to please him. During the first few months of their marriage, their matings had been frequent and quick, Tyler always assuring her that she'd satisfied him completely. But he had lied. She had never satisfied him any more than he had her. Seldom had he given her pleasure, and in less than a year after they had taken vows to be faithful until death, Tyler was bedding other women. If only she'd been brave enough to face that truth long ago.

Lydia couldn't understand why Wade Cameron evoked such strong emotions in her, such primitive sexual desire. She had never wanted a man the way she wanted him. The erotic fantasies that kept playing over and over in her mind were driving her crazy.

She placed her hand at her throat and ran it down her neck, onto her chest, slipping it inside her satin robe. Running her hand across her breasts, over her nipples, Lydia felt her body respond. God, she had to stop this! She had to stop thinking about Wade. She had to stop dreaming of what it would be like if they made love.

She sat down on the bed, dropping her head, covering her face with her hands as she tried not to cry. Then she heard the noise. There was a car pulling into her driveway. No, she told herself, not a car—a truck.

Jumping up, she stood by the bed and wiped away the teardrops from the corner of her eyes. She pulled her robe tightly closed, readjusting the belt until it bit into her waist.

What was Wade doing coming here tonight? At one-thirty in the morning on New Year's Day? Before she could begin to make sense of his arrival, Lydia heard the doorbell ring. Cupping her hands in front of her mouth, she sucked in a deep breath, then let it out. Did she dare open the front door to him? If she did, what would happen?

Barefooted and wearing only her bikini panties and silk robe, Lydia walked out of her bedroom, down the stairs and toward the front door. She stopped in the middle of the foyer, unable to go any farther. He kept ringing the doorbell over and over again. Obviously, he was determined to see her.

Suddenly the ringing stopped and the pounding began. She realized he was beating on the door with his fist.

"Lydia, I know you're in there. Come to the door, dammit."

Oh, mercy, he was shouting. His bellowing could waken the neighbors, alert Glenn and Eloise to his presence. She prayed they hadn't already heard the sound of his truck when he'd pulled into the driveway. If the neighbors heard anything, the news that Lydia had had a late-night visitor would be all over town by morning.

Awakened by the noise, Leo came bounding out of his bed in the den and ran into the foyer. Growling, the fuzzy puppy jumped in front of Lydia, eyeing the front door and emitting several fierce barks.

Reaching down to pet him on the head, Lydia whispered, "Hush, Leo. It's all right."

Her assurance silenced him, but he remained at her side. Hesitantly she turned on the overhead light in the foyer. Holding her breath, she prayed Wade would go away and leave her alone. Tonight, she was lonely and vulnerable, and her will to resist was disappearing fast.

He pounded on the door again. Harder. Louder. Leo growled.

"I'm not leaving until I see you," Wade yelled.

Practically running, Lydia hurried across the foyer, grabbed the brass doorknob and swung open the stained-glass and wooden front door. Wade Cameron stood on her porch, his hair and jacket covered with melting snow-flakes. He hung in the doorway, his body slightly bent, one big hand resting on the door frame. He gazed at her with those black, black eyes, and she felt a quickening in her body from her breasts to the apex between her thighs. She'd never seen anything as beautiful as the big, dark man hovering in her doorway and looking at her with such undisguised hunger.

Wade assessed her body from the top of her head to the bottom of her bare feet. Her hair hung loosely, just touching her shoulders, and nothing but an almost transparent silk robe covered her slender body. He'd been aroused for hours, and just the sight of her made his body throb with a need that had to be sated soon or he'd die. Never, in his thirty-two years, had he ever seen anything as beautiful as the woman standing just inside the doorway, looking up at him, undeniable yearning in her warm hazel eyes.

She opened her mouth to speak, but no sound came out. The freezing January wind seeped through her flimsy robe, chilling her, making her tremble. Somewhere in the distance a train whistle blew and a lone dog barked. Suddenly

Leo yelped twice, then moved forward to crouch at Lydia's knee. He sniffed at Wade, then wagged his tail.

Neither human paid any attention to the animal, who stood guard at Lydia's side. All Lydia could see was Wade. All Wade could see was Lydia.

"Lydia," he said in a whispering voice, deep, dark and agonized.

"You shouldn't . . . shouldn't be here."

He stood up straight, never taking his eyes off her face. "Don't send me away," he said.

Some restraining barrier inside Lydia crumbled, and she stepped backward into the foyer to make room for his entrance.

Without saying a word he stepped over the threshold and into Lydia Reid's home, then slammed the door behind him. He unzipped his jacket, ran an unsteady hand through his damp hair and made a tentative move toward her.

The sound of the slamming door reverberated in her ears like a cannon blast, alerting her to the finality of the decision she'd made by allowing him inside her home. All she needed to have done to end things with this man once and for all was send him away tonight. It should have been simple, but it wasn't. She knew what she had done was wrong, that she had sealed her fate by not turning him away.

When he took another step toward her, Lydia backed up. Leo sniffed at Wade before ambling back toward the den. The soft overhead light in the foyer gave Wade a perfect view of Lydia where she stood in the shadows with the dark hallway leading into the kitchen and den directly behind her.

When Wade moved forward, Lydia, still facing him, began to retreat, slowly, carefully walking backward. She couldn't allow him to get near her. If he touched her, she knew she'd be lost. She had wanted him too much and for too long. She stared at him, noticing every detail of his appearance, from the top of his wet black curls to the tips of his damp, scuffed boots. He was watching her with a degree of intensity that matched hers, and his lustful appraisal sent shivers racing through her.

Spots of moisture dotted his brown leather jacket and tight, faded jeans. The top three buttons of his gray flannel shirt were undone just enough to reveal a swirl of thick black chest hair. Lydia allowed her gaze to travel over him, taking in the desire in his dark eyes, the determined set of his jaw, the thick muscles in his chest and the straining bulge in his jeans.

When he realized how uneasy she felt, he stopped and simply stared at her while she surveyed him from head to toe. Damn, but she looked even better than he'd remembered. And, of course, he'd never seen her in so few clothes. That sheer ivory robe, although it was long sleeved and skimmed the floor, did little to conceal the ripe curves hidden beneath its fragile cover. He could see the outline of her high, full breasts, the hint of pink nipples, the shadow of a tiny navel, and the lacy ruffles on her bikini panties.

He grew even more aroused and he groaned from the need, building inside him. He wanted Lydia, and, by heaven, he meant to have her.

He took another step in her direction. She backed up until she moved into the dark hallway. Wade followed, pushing her up against the closed kitchen door. She stood rigidly, her heart beating loud and wild. He braced both his big hands on the door frame on each side of her, then lowered his head so that his breath mingled with hers.

"You can't run from this," he said, his lips almost touching hers. "Neither of us can escape what's between us."

"Wade." His name erupted from her lips like a shot of hot lava escaping from a dormant volcano on the brink of exploding.

"Yes. Dammit, yes!" He covered her mouth with his own, taking her soft lips between his teeth, nipping, licking, tasting. Deepening the kiss, he thrust his tongue into her welcoming warmth, allowing himself free rein while she sought to match his ravaging with feminine strokes of her own.

He grabbed her by the shoulders and pulled her away from the door and into his arms. She went willingly, throwing her arms around his neck, silently pleading while her body molded itself to his. Her response was the answer to his prayers. He'd dreamed of this, longed for this for months. Perhaps, if he were brave enough to tell the truth, he would have to admit that he'd wanted to make love to Lydia Reid since the night they'd met at the hospital nearly nine months ago.

He couldn't kiss her enough—the taste of her was driving him crazy. So sweet, so warm and alive. She groaned into his mouth when he ran his big hands down her back, cupping her buttocks and pulling her up against his arousal. Instinctively she tried to move closer. Her body trembled with primitive need, compelling her to submit to his masculine dominance, his predatory right to claim her as his mate.

She slid her hands down his chest, around and inside his jacket, then back up to his shoulders. With slow, steady movements, she eased his jacket off and let it drop to the floor. She wanted his chest bare, his thickly muscled body and curling hair available for the pleasure her fingertips sought to find.

One by one, she undid the buttons on his shirt while he massaged her hips and buttocks through the thin layer of silk that covered them. She slipped his shirt off, letting it fall to the floor. Frustrated by the barrier his V-necked T-shirt created, Lydia tried to pull the garment over his head, and cried out when it caught around his big shoulders. Tugging fiercely, she managed to free the T-shirt, baring his chest. Lydia closed her eyes and breathed in the uniquely masculine aroma that was Wade's alone. With shaky fingers, she stroked his chest, from his broad shoulders to his narrow waist. When she moved her hands to his belt, he grabbed her wrists and pushed her up against the wall.

"I can't take much more of this," he panted. "I've got to take you."

"Yes," she moaned when he loosened her belt. "I want you."

Her robe hung open, the lapels caught on the upward tilt of her breasts. Her bikini panties dipped low in front, a wide band of lace decorating the edge. Brushing aside the robe, he covered one breast with his hot mouth while he slipped his fingers inside the waistband of her panties. While his mouth sucked greedily at her breast, he edged her panties down her hips, down her legs and over her feet.

Wade knelt down. Moving his big hands up her calves, he caressed her smooth skin, petted the outer curve of her thighs and massaged her hips. Slipping his hand between her legs, Wade stroked her inner thighs, soothing her with his touch until the sensations began to fan the fires of desire blazing within her.

She whimpered. Her knees bolted and she swayed. Wade braced her body with one big hand placed around her waist. When he palmed her softly, she cried with need, holding him to her.

With his patience at an end, Wade stood and pressed Lydia against the wall, kissing her neck, her chin, then taking her lips again. He undid his belt, unzipped his jeans and shed the remainder of his clothes with one swift downward tug. Kicking the garments aside, he scooped Lydia's hips into his big hands, spreading her legs and bracing her against the wall. She cried out when he pulled her legs around him, driving into her with one strong, hard stab.

She clung to him, her mouth seeking and finding his. While he plunged into her repeatedly, rocking her body back and forth onto his, he murmured hot, sexy words of praise and intent. When he told her how it felt to be buried deep inside her, Lydia trembled, her entire consciousness focused on the swelling intensity building in the apex between her thighs.

He could feel her tightening around him, shivering, nearing release. Quickening the depth and intensity of his thrusts, Wade moaned two sizzling words into her ear, and she exploded around him. Her cries of fulfillment permeated the quiet stillness of the house.

Her climactic shudders raced through him. With one final, triumphant lunge, Wade emptied himself into her receptive body. They clung to each other, hot and wet and trembling with the pleasure of sating a desire too long denied.

Ever so slowly, Wade lowered Lydia's legs downward until her feet touched the floor. He held her against him, her tight, swollen breasts brushing across his damp chest, her erect nipples lost in his chest hair.

"You're wonderful, Lydia," he said, his lips on hers. "So wonderful."

"No, you're wonderful," she said, and made no protest when he picked her up in his arms, carried her down the hallway and up the stairs.

Several hours later Lydia lay alone in her bed. She heard the sound of Wade's truck engine starting. It wasn't daylight yet, so there was a slight chance that no one would see him leave. She realized it was a little late to be worrying about someone finding out that Wade Cameron had come to her house at one-thirty in the morning and had stayed for nearly four hours.

The time she had spent with Wade, although just ended, seemed like some erotic dream, far too good to have actually happened, and yet far too satisfying not to have been real. She realized now that she had never made love before, that what she'd shared with Tyler hadn't even come close to the real thing. There was something so raw and primitive in what she'd known with Wade—steamy, smoldering sex.

After he'd carried her upstairs, she'd pointed the way to her bedroom, not once thinking about the times she'd been with Tyler in the very same bed. Wade had laid her down, and with slow, torturing strokes, covered every inch of her body with his hands and lips, his tongue teaching her new meaning of the word *worship*.

When he'd brought her to fulfillment, she'd gone wild in his arms, longing to give him the same satisfaction. When he forced her to slow down, she fought him until he told her that he needed to hear her cries of completion again before he could be satisfied.

They had slept briefly, both sated and exhausted. He had awakened first and begun caressing her. She'd accepted him for the third time, unmindful that she was already sore, her nipples overly sensitive and her body aching from Wade's forceful loving.

The final time had been as hot and wild and exciting as the first time. Lydia suspected that it could always be that way between them.

He'd told her he wanted to see her again, that he thought the two of them were good for each other. He'd reacted with typical macho anger when she'd told him that she couldn't have an affair with him, that she was, officially, still in mourning for Tyler, and that the only kind of relationship she wanted was marriage.

He'd made it abundantly clear that he wasn't in the market for a wife. Not now. Probably not ever. Macie had soured him on marriage and taught him not to trust women in general.

Wade had argued with her, had tried to convince her that no matter how hard they tried, they'd never be able to stay away from each other. When he'd stormed out of her bedroom, he'd shouted at her that he wouldn't be back, that the next time she'd have to come to him.

She wanted Wade, more than she'd ever thought it possible to want a man. He'd given her so much besides physical pleasure. He had taught her what a sensual woman she was, and had given back to her some of the pride Tyler had taken from her by his repeated infidelities.

But Wade Cameron wouldn't be able to function in her world any more than she would be able to function in his. In her world, young widows didn't have affairs with men not on their social level. Marriage, of course, was out of the question. He would never move to town and live off her money, and she could never live on a run-down farm with his mother and daughter.

There was only one solution. Tonight would have to be a once-in-a-lifetime memory. In the weeks ahead she would have to rebuild her life. And she'd have to do it without Wade Cameron.

Seven

———

Lydia turned off the thirteen-inch portable television sitting on the kitchen counter. She placed her empty coffee cup in the sink and looked out the window, watching the swirling gray clouds that obscured the morning sun and shadowed the earth with gloomy light. No doubt the local weatherman's prediction of rain turning into light sleet would become a reality by late afternoon. All the more reason for her to get ready and go out to the farm before noon, she decided. No need to take any chances with February weather in Mississippi. It could be too unpredictable.

She hadn't seen Wade Cameron in over six weeks, but today she would have to face him. She realized that she had other choices, that she could leave Riverton and no one would ever know, that she could keep her secret—maybe forever.

Lydia was surprised that Eloise hadn't mentioned hearing or seeing Wade's truck at her house on New Year's Day, but Glenn's mother had never said a word. Perhaps the champagne Eloise drank at the country club party explained why she'd slept through Wade's visit. Whatever the reason, Lydia had been grateful that the gossip about Wade and her had died down. As far as she knew no one in Riverton was aware of what had happened New Year's morning. No one except the mysterious caller. The voice had told Lydia that she was making a big mistake starting an affair with a dirt poor, redneck farmer, and had gone on to warn her to break it off immediately. There had been only one threatening call, on the second of January. What would happen, Lydia wondered, when the caller learned her secret?

Lydia had been determined to set her life on a new course after her tempestuous night with Wade, and each day she'd taken a step forward toward the future. She had distributed over half of Tyler's legacy to charity and was using part of it to rebuild her interior design business. She'd decided to begin by working out of her home, and already had two clients, one a newlywed decorating her first home, the other a local lawyer and his wife who were remodeling.

Walking through the den, Lydia glanced at the worktable in the corner of the room. Wallpaper, carpet and paint swatches were neatly arranged in fan-shaped patterns. Her portfolios were stacked against the wall. Her personal directory of wholesale dealers lay beside the phone.

Glaring at the telephone, she reached down, her hand shaking as she picked up the receiver. *Dial the number,* she told herself. *Call him and tell him you have to talk to him— today.* One by one, she punched out the numbers and listened for the ring.

Clutching the phone tightly, she drew in a steadying breath when she heard Ruthie Cameron's voice. "Hello."

Lydia slammed the phone down, her hands trembling, moisture coating her upper lip. She couldn't talk to him over the phone. She had to see him in person.

After what had happened between them on New Year's morning, she'd known she had to avoid him at any cost. Although she freely admitted to herself that she was half in love with Wade Cameron and that she missed him terribly, she knew they had no future together. So during the past six weeks, she had begun to put her life in order and tried to forget the desire she felt for a man so totally unsuitable for her.

But yesterday, after her appointment with a doctor in Corinth, she knew she couldn't plan her future without Wade.

Wade noticed the blue BMW parked in the driveway the minute he drove in from the fields. He'd spent hours checking the cattle and feed blocks, distributing the hay and making sure the fences were sturdy. With the weather the way it was, he had to make sure his herd was safe and well cared for.

Maneuvering the truck around to the side of the house, he turned off the ignition and sat there staring at Lydia Reid's car. Gripping the steering wheel in his hands, he cursed, then bent over, resting his forehead against his knuckles. What the hell was she doing here? he wondered. Six weeks ago she'd made it plain that she never wanted to see him again. It had been the longest six weeks of his life.

He hadn't seen her since the night they'd made love, since the night she'd gone wild in his arms. Every time he thought about her, which was every single day, he got hard and hot. He'd never wanted a woman the way he had wanted Lydia, the way he still did.

There had been more than enough going on in his life to keep him busy, but alone in his bed at night a tawny-haired temptress with bright hazel eyes crept into his thoughts and kept him awake for hours. He remembered everything about her. The way she smelled, all flowery and feminine. The way her skin felt beneath his fingertips, all soft and silky. The way she tasted, so sweet and moist. The way she sounded, those wild moans of pleasure when he'd been buried deep inside her.

You can't sit here in the truck all day, he told himself. *Sooner or later, you're going to have to go inside and face her.* Maybe she wasn't even here to see him. Maybe she'd come to see his mother. It was possible that Glenn Haraway had sent her to talk to Ruthie about selling her Cotton Row property.

He'd heard rumors that Lydia had been seeing a lot of ol' friend-of-the-family. Tanya had said that folks were taking odds on how soon after her year of mourning ended Lydia would marry the new mayor. The very thought of Glenn Haraway touching Lydia shot Wade's blood pressure sky high and angered him to the point of wanting to do physical harm to the other man.

Even though he knew Haraway was more suitable as husband material for Lydia than a guy like him, he couldn't believe that she'd marry a man she didn't love. Hell, she came closer to loving him than she did Haraway. He'd bet every dime he had that she hadn't made love with her next-door neighbor.

Picking up his cap from the seat, Wade opened the truck door and stepped outside. Cold rain mixed with light sleet pelted his face. With long, quick strides, he rounded the house and entered the back porch. He hesitated briefly when he heard voices coming from the kitchen. His mother was entertaining their guest in the kitchen! Wade grunted, wondering what Lydia thought of Ruthie Cameron's country manners.

"Well, there he is," Ruthie said when Wade opened the back door. "I was about to send somebody out to look for you."

Wade wiped his feet on the braided rug just outside the door, then took off his cap and work coat. He didn't want to turn around and look at her. He was too afraid of how he'd feel, of what he might say or do.

"Don't dawdle there, boy." Ruthie got up from the table, took down a ceramic mug from the cabinet and poured a cup of coffee. "Mrs. Reid's been waiting to see you for nearly an hour."

When he glanced in Lydia's direction, she stared down at her clasped hands resting in her lap. "You're here to see me?" he asked.

Ruthie handed her son the mug of hot coffee. "Sit down. You must be near froze to death."

"Thanks." Wade accepted the mug, but didn't sit down.

"It's been nice visiting with you, Lydia," Ruthie said, smiling. "I got me some mending to do, so I'll just go watch my soap opera while you two have your talk."

Lydia looked as if she'd been crying, Wade thought. Her eyes were overly bright and circled with dark shadows. But she was beautiful. As beautiful sitting here in the farmhouse kitchen as she'd been in her own bedroom. As gorgeous and desirable in her navy and green plaid slacks and red sweater as she'd been in an ivory silk robe.

"I didn't ever expect to see you again, and certainly never out here at the farm." He set the mug on the table, pulled out a chair and sat down across from her.

Lydia couldn't bring herself to face him. With her gaze cast downward, she replied, "I wouldn't be here if it weren't important."

"Yeah, well, when I saw your car parked outside, I figured Haraway had sent you out here to talk to Ma." Wade cradled the mug in his hands, watching the steam rise off the hot liquid.

"This visit has nothing to do with Glenn or the new mall. It's personal." She forced herself to look up and into Wade's black eyes.

Her breathing quickened, her heartbeat accelerated and the bottom dropped out of her stomach. He was staring at her as if she were a stranger. Perhaps what they'd shared hadn't meant as much to him as it had to her.

"Sounds serious." Wade dipped two spoonfuls of sugar into his coffee. "You didn't come all the way out here to issue me an invitation to the wedding, did you?"

Lydia's face paled. "What wedding? What are you talking about?"

"My sister-in-law told me that everybody's eagerly waiting for you and Haraway to announce your engagement." Wade stirred his coffee, set the spoon down on the table and picked up his mug.

"That's the most ridiculous thing I've ever heard. Glenn and I are friends. He . . . he was Tyler's best friend."

Wade took a couple of sips from his coffee. "Then why are you here, Lydia?" He watched her, noticing the way her eyes had misted, the way she tightly clutched her hands in front of her, the way her bottom lip quivered. "I thought we agreed it was best for both of us if we didn't see each other again."

"We did."

"Then why—"

"There's something I think you should know." Lydia scooted the chair away from the table and stood.

"I'm listening."

"I want you to know that I almost didn't come to you, that I considered leaving town, going back to Birmingham."

A tight knot formed in the pit of his stomach. "Just what are you trying to say?"

"I'm pregnant. Six weeks pregnant."

He'd known before the words were out of her mouth. He'd known. He'd lost his head that night, he'd gone to her house unprepared, and he'd taken her three times in a wild frenzy without any thought of protection. He hadn't been such a fool in years, not since Macie had trapped him into marriage with a lie, a lie about being pregnant.

"You're sure?" Wade wondered if she was lying? Could she have some ulterior motive for coming to him with this pregnancy story? Macie had tricked him into marriage. What did Lydia really want?

"I drove over to Corinth yesterday and saw a doctor there." Lydia couldn't bear seeing the doubt in his eyes.

Dear God, he didn't believe her. Did he actually think she'd put herself through this humiliation if she weren't one hundred percent sure?

"Didn't want anybody in town to suspect?" Maybe she *was* pregnant, he thought. Maybe it was Haraway's kid... Hell and damnation, if she was pregnant, the child wasn't Haraway's, Wade told himself. He knew damn well it was his. Lydia wasn't the kind of woman who'd be bedding two men at the same time.

"When I explained to the doctor that I wasn't married, he explained my options."

"Abortion?"

"That and adoption and becoming a single parent."

"You can't stay on in Riverton and have a baby out of wedlock. The good people would burn you at the stake." Here it comes, he thought. She's going to tell me what she wants from me. She'll probably cry. Macie had cried when she'd told him she was pregnant. Six months later she really had been pregnant, with Molly, but not the night she'd come to him in tears, the night she'd lied to him. He'd married her, not loving her, because of that lie and they'd spent the next six years in a living hell.

"You don't care?" Lydia didn't understand how he could act so nonchalant. It was as if he didn't believe her, as if he didn't think they could have created a child together.

"What do you want from me?" He sipped on his coffee, eyeing her over the top of the mug.

"I don't want anything, Wade." She gripped the back of the wooden kitchen chair. "I simply thought that as the father you had a right to know."

"Do you want marriage?"

Her mouth opened on a gasp, tears filling her eyes.

A part of Wade wanted to reach out and pull her into his arms. The smarter part of him said, "You don't want marriage, huh? What about child support, starting today? Or maybe you'd like Ma to sign over the deed to the Cotton Row property."

Tears streamed down her face. She licked them off her lips, wiped them off her cheeks and blinked them from her eyes. "Why are you acting like this? What's the matter with you? The only reason I came out here today was to tell you that I'm pregnant because... because I thought you had a right to know. Why don't you believe me?"

"That's just it, sweetheart. I don't believe you." He pushed the chair back, stood and took several steps toward her. "One woman lied to me about being pregnant. She wanted me to marry her, and I did. I swore I'd never be gullible enough to get caught in that trap again."

"I'm not asking for marriage. I don't need you or anything you have." She glared at him. Shaking with anger as she stepped closer, their bodies separated by only a few inches. "You big idiot." She jabbed her finger into his chest. "I've got more money that you'll ever have. And as far as your mother's Cotton Row property, well, I... I don't give a damn. Not about the property, and not about the new mall."

He stared at her, stunned by her outburst of anger, shocked that she'd defend her actions by attacking him. Without thinking he grabbed her by the shoulders, shaking her soundly. "Don't lie to me. You want something."

She tried to free herself from his tenacious hold. "Let go of me."

He stopped shaking her, pulled her into his arms and lowered his head. "Damn you." Then he kissed her, a possessive, punishing kiss. Wade felt his body responding, and knew he wanted her just as much as ever.

She jerked away from him, stepping backward, her eyes glazed with drying tears. "I promise you that I won't bother you again. I'm not sure whether I'll stay on in Riverton or move somewhere else, but you can be assured that neither I nor my baby will ever cause any problems for you."

Lydia rushed out of the kitchen, picking up her purse and coat off the pine coatrack in the hallway. She opened the front door.

"Lydia." Wade followed, then stopped right behind her.

"I would never lie to you, Wade," she said, her back to him. When he took her by the shoulders, she jerked forward, pulling away from him and stepping out onto the front porch.

When he called her name again, she ran down the steps and out to her car. Icy rain fell from a sooty gray sky. A cold north wind swayed the trees and whipped through the dead grass and weeds. With tears blurring her vision, with anger and frustration pulsing through her quaking body, Lydia drove down the long gravel lane leading from the Cameron farm to the state road.

She wasn't sure what she'd expected when she'd come here today, but one thing was for sure—she'd gotten more than she'd bargained for. At this precise moment she hated Wade Cameron more than she loved him, and she hoped she never saw him again as long as she lived.

"You just gonna let her leave like that?" Ruthie Cameron walked out of the living room, a threaded needle and a darned sock in her hands.

"Were you listening?" Wade slammed the front door and turned to confront his mother.

"I'd have had to be deaf not to have heard you two." Ruthie laid her mending down on the pine table by the staircase. "You gave that gal a pretty hard time."

"She tried to make me believe she's pregnant." Wade ran his fingers through his hair while he paced up and down the hallway. "I'm not stupid enough to make the same mistake twice."

"No, but you're stupid enough to make a fool of yourself."

"What?" He jerked around, giving his mother a hard, condemning look.

"The gal that just left here with her heart broken ain't Macie. She's Lydia Reid. A woman who swallowed her pride to come out here and tell you she's carrying your baby. A woman who cares enough about you to think you had a right to know the truth.''

"The truth? Hmph..."

"Yeah, boy, the truth, only you're too big a fool to know it." Ruthie disappeared into the kitchen, returning quickly carrying Wade's dress hat and coat.

"What the—"

"Don't you cuss at me, Wade Hoyt Cameron." Ruthie handed her son his hat and coat. "You go get Lydia. You ask her to forgive you for acting like a jackass. Then you two talk things over, decide what you ought to do for yourselves and that new grandbaby of mine.''

Without saying another word Wade slipped into his coat and set his Stetson on his head. Good God in heaven, why had he treated Lydia the way he had? His mother was right. Lydia Reid would never have lied to him about being pregnant. When she'd told him, all he could think about was Macie, about the lies he'd believed, about the pain he'd endured because he'd once been so young and gullible.

Wade opened the front door and rushed outside. Ruthie followed him onto the front porch.

"You drive careful. That rain's almost pure sleet now," Ruthie said.

He wasn't listening to his mother's warning when he jumped in his truck and headed toward the state road. He couldn't see Lydia's BMW. That meant she had to be driving too fast.

By the time he caught up with her she was halfway into town, and he'd been right. She was driving too fast. In a hurry to get away from him, no doubt. Well, he didn't blame her. He'd said some pretty awful things to her.

When Wade noticed how slick the road had become and the way ice was forming on the trees and power lines, he figured the temperature had been dropping fast. He honked the horn, hoping Lydia would pull off the road. She had no business driving in this weather. She should have called and asked him to come into town today instead of risking an accident by driving out to the farm.

When she made no move to stop, Wade honked the horn again. This time she speeded up. Dammit, she had to be hurt and angry, and he was probably the last person on earth she wanted to see. But didn't she realize that it was dangerous to go any faster on the icy road?

Looking up the highway as far as visibility permitted, Wade didn't see any other vehicle moving in their direction. Pressing down on the accelerator, he maneuvered the truck into the oncoming lane, pulling up beside Lydia's car. He honked the horn again.

He glanced over just as she turned her head toward the side window. Her eyes were swollen and red, her face wet with tears. The knot in his stomach tightened. He'd done that to her, he told himself.

When he motioned for her to stop, she shook her head and kept driving. He slowed down and pulled the truck in behind her BMW, deciding he would just follow her into town since she seemed determined not to pull over.

Suddenly Lydia increased her speed and the BMW flew away, leaving Wade behind. Hell! What was she trying to do, kill herself? Wade fumed, then increased the speed of his truck as much as he deemed safe.

He saw it all as if in slow motion, and yet it happened so quickly that it was over in a matter of seconds. The BMW skidded, did a fast half turn and plunged into a deep ditch on the other side of the road.

Wade's heartbeat thundered in his ears. All he could think about was Lydia. Getting to her. Making sure she was all right.

He swerved the truck to the left. The tires slid across the same icy patch in the road Lydia's car had obviously hit. Pulling his truck off the road directly behind her BMW, Wade swung open the door and hopped out. He ran down the steep embankment, rushed over to Lydia's car and jerked open the door. She sat slumped over the air bag, her head resting in her hands.

"What the hell did you think you were doing?" he yelled.

She turned her head and looked up at him. "I was trying to get as far away from you as I could get."

He reached inside the car, placing one arm behind her back, taking her hands in his to assist her up and out of the wrecked car. She glared at him, but accepted his help.

"I suppose you'll have to drive me into town," she said, pulling away from him the minute she stood on her own two feet. "I'll call a wrecker from the house."

When he tried to help her up the embankment, she slapped his hands away. He grunted, shaking his head in bewilderment.

When they reached his truck, he walked around to the passenger side and opened the door for her. She took one step upward, swayed slightly, then fell backward right into Wade's arms. She felt as limp as a dishrag, he thought, then took a good look at her closed eyes and shallow breathing and realized that she'd fainted. Lifting her into the truck, he laid her across the seat, then ran around and got in the other side.

"Hang on, honey. I'll get you to the hospital." Wade had never been so scared in all his life.

Wade felt like a caged animal as he paced back and forth in the emergency room waiting area. Stopping in front of the automatic double doors leading onto the parking lot, he looked outside, seeing icicles hanging from the roof's edge, a glazed icy coating over the black pavement and a gray sky filled with charcoal clouds.

Ten months ago he'd run through these very same doors on the night Macie had died. So much had happened in those brief ten months. He had met Lydia Reid. He had wanted her to the point of madness, and finally he'd taken her. And now she was pregnant.

He could kick himself for treating her so badly when she'd come to him with the news. Hell, he'd mauled her feelings, destroying any fondness she might have had for him. He knew he'd acted like a fool. He had lashed out at her, venting all the anger and hatred he'd felt for Macie toward Lydia, who, he reminded himself, had been innocent of any sins against him. Macie had tricked him into marriage over seven years ago, and by the time he realized she hadn't been pregnant as she'd claimed, she was already nearly two months along with Molly. His little girl was the only decent thing that came out of his relationship with his former wife. He loved his child, and if Lydia gave him the chance, he'd prove to her that he could love the child she carried.

What if she loses the baby? he agonized, berating himself for chasing after Lydia like a half-crazed idiot. Why had he kept honking at her, motioning for her to pull over? He could have just followed her home and then confronted her. But no, he had pressured her into running—running her car straight into a ditch.

For the six years of his loveless marriage to Macie, he'd been the brunt of other men's jokes and the object of his friends' and family's pity. His wife had been the best-known slut in Riverton. A man didn't forget things like that. Not in ten months. Hell, not in ten years or a lifetime. But, as Ma had pointed out, Lydia wasn't Macie, and he had no right blaming one woman for another's sins.

After today Riverton would be buzzing with the news that Lydia had been brought into the hospital by Wade Cameron after she'd had a wreck coming home from his house. And worst of all the news that she was pregnant was sure to leak out. By morning they were bound to be the talk of the town all over again. God, she'd hate that, and there wasn't anything either of them could do to squelch the rumors.

"Mr. Cameron?" A tall, stout nurse stood in the doorway leading back into the examining rooms.

Wade rushed over to her. "Is Lydia all right? Can I see her?"

"Dr. Bickly has finished his examination. He wants to speak to you. Go right on back."

The slender, bespectacled man, whom Wade had seen with Lydia the night of Tyler's death, stood just outside an oval office area where several nurses were busily attending to their duties.

Dr. Bickly held out his hand. "Mr. Cameron?"

Wade shook the doctor's hand. "How is she?"

"Lydia is fine, just a little shaken after the accident. And it's not uncommon for pregnant women to faint."

"Is there any problem with the baby?" Wade saw no condemnation in the other man's eyes.

"Neither Lydia nor her child received any physical injury in the wreck, but Lydia's emotional state is another matter."

"She's upset." Wade knew she had every right to be mad as blue blazes, to want to rip off a few inches of his hide, but he'd make it up to her—if only she'd let him.

"She told me she went to a doctor in Corinth to confirm her pregnancy, instead of coming to me, because she knew that word would leak out. Someone would see her in my office, or even one of my staff might accidentally mention it to a friend or relative."

"She's always been too concerned about what other people think." Wade had the urge to go in there, give her a sound shake, and tell her that from now on she wasn't to give a damn what anyone else thought about her.

"It's the way she was raised," Dr. Bickly said. "Have you ever met her mother?"

"No."

Dr. Bickly rubbed the back of his neck, then shrugged his shoulders. "Well, Lydia wants to see you, young man, so you better go on back there." He pointed one long, bony finger directly at Wade. "But don't you upset her."

Wade hesitated momentarily outside the door, knocked once, then walked in. She had dressed and sat in a chair beside the examining table. Although she looked tired and disheveled, Wade thought she was the most beautiful sight he'd ever seen.

"The doctor said that you're okay. And the baby, too." He closed the door behind him, but made no attempt to reach out and pull her into his arms, even though that was exactly what he wanted to do.

"I wanted to talk to you before I call Glenn to come and take me home."

"You don't have to call Haraway. I'll take you home."

."No. I think you made your feelings perfectly clear earlier today out at the farm."

"I was wrong. I wasn't thinking straight. In my mind I had you all mixed up with Macie."

When he saw her wince as if in pain, he regretted his choice of words. "What I'm trying to say is that once I'd cooled off, I realized that you wouldn't lie to me."

"How nice of you to believe me." She stiffened her back, sat up ramrod straight and thrust out her chin.

"There's no getting around the fact that we're going to be the talk of the town again. I know you'll hate it, but it's inevitable. I can't do anything to stop it, but I know one damn sure way to really give them something to talk about."

"I'm going to leave Riverton." She stood up, holding her head high. She walked over to where he stood by the door.

"You damn well aren't leaving." He glared at her, daring her to try to move past him.

"I suppose you have another solution?"

"Yeah, I do. We're getting married."

"What?" Lydia reached out, balancing herself by gripping a nearby metal table.

"I said we're getting married. As soon as possible."

Eight

The first week of March they were married by Judge Franklin, one of Lydia's personal friends. Two courthouse employees acted as witnesses. The entire ceremony lasted less than five minutes. In the ten days since her accident Lydia had reviewed, again and again, all the reasons why she shouldn't marry Wade Cameron, all the reasons why a marriage between the two of them would be doomed from the start. But in the final analysis two single factors tilted the scales in favor of a lifetime commitment. First, she was two months pregnant with his child. Second, she had garnered the courage to admit to herself that she was in love with him.

"We're here," Wade said as he parked his truck in the front drive. "Brace yourself. Ma's probably planned some sort of celebration."

After getting out of the truck, he went around to the passenger side and helped Lydia. She looked beautiful in her winter-beige suit and matching hat, the veil just touching her nose. But she definitely wasn't the picture of a happy bride.

Her face was too pale, her smile too forced and her eyes lacked their usual sparkle.

"Your mother's been very kind," Lydia said, stepping up onto the front porch. "I know I'm not the woman she would have chosen for you."

Wade stepped up beside her, hesitating before opening the front door. "Ma's not the type to butt in to our business. She'll do right by you if you do right by her."

Lydia glanced at Wade, her somber groom, who looked uncomfortable in his black suit, white shirt and dark striped tie. She wished he looked happier, but why should he? For the second time in his life, he had married a woman for all the wrong reasons. "I'll try to be a good mother to Molly. I'm quite fond of her and I think she likes me."

"Molly likes you just fine, but there's no need for you to put yourself out trying to be her mother." Wade opened the door and stood back, waiting for Lydia to enter. "About all the mothering she's ever had came from Ma."

Lydia realized that Wade hadn't meant to hurt her feelings, but he had. How could they hope to have a normal marriage if he didn't even want her to make an effort at being a mother to his little girl?

Just as they walked into the hallway, Ruthie Cameron, dressed in a plain brown dress and her sensible lace-up shoes, came out of the living room. She opened her fat arms, embracing both Wade and Lydia in one hug.

"Welcome home." Ruthie's smile was warm and genuine. "Come on in." Placing her son beside her on the left and his bride beside her on the right, Ruthie led them into the living room. "Tanya and Britt's come over, and I let Molly stay home from school for the special occasion."

Molly, wearing a flowery-print dress, white socks and black patent leather shoes, came running up to Lydia. "I wanted to come to the wedding, but Daddy wouldn't let me."

Lydia gave Wade a sideways glance, then focused her attention on his daughter. "It wasn't anything fancy, so all you missed was the two of us exchanging our vows in front of the judge in his chambers at the courthouse."

"Well, they're home now, girlie," Ruthie said. "And you're here for the celebration. Come on in the kitchen and help me with the cake."

"I'll bring you the biggest piece, Lydia," Molly said, giving her father a pouty look. "And I'll take pieces outside for Bear and Rawhide and Leo. I think Leo's going to like living on a farm."

"Y'all go on and sit down and talk to Britt and Tanya. Me and Molly can take care of the refreshments." Ruthie waddled across the room, Molly already ahead of her.

Lydia sat down in a colonial-style recliner, covered in a hideous orange plaid material that was threadbare on the arms and the seat. Wade sat down on the couch next to his brother.

"Ma's given me strict instructions to keep my opinions to myself," Britt said.

"When have Ma's warnings ever stopped you from saying whatever you wanted?" Wade asked.

"Please, Britt, don't." Tanya, who was sitting in a straight-backed wooden chair beside the couch, reached over and touched her husband on the arm.

Britt jerked his arm away, and at that moment Lydia thought she'd never seen a more dangerous man in all her life. She suspected that there was an agony inside Britt Cameron, a pent-up rage, just waiting to burst loose.

"Welcome to the Cameron family," Tanya said. "Ma's a dear, and you'll like Lily and Amy when you meet them, though there's no telling when those two will be making a visit."

"I hope you and I can become friends." Lydia liked her new sister-in-law, although the younger woman seemed a bit immature. There was something sweet and vulnerable about Tanya Cameron, almost as if she were an unloved child.

"I'm counting on it," Tanya said. "Ma's good company, but she's not much for running into town and driving down to Tupelo or over to Corinth for shopping and stuff."

"I love to shop, and I'll have to be making occasional trips out of town. I've been working on rebuilding my interior design firm. I have two clients and hope to have many more in the future."

"Are you going to let your wife run around all over creation while she's pregnant?" Britt asked his brother.

"She won't be—"

"Wade and I haven't had a chance to discuss my work," Lydia said.

"I think it's wonderful that you've got a career." Tanya got up when she saw Molly walk in carrying a tray of cake slices. "I got married . . . the first time . . . right out of high school. Never had a chance to go on to college or anything." She took the tray from Molly. "Here, honey, let me help you with that."

"I want to give Lydia her piece." Molly grabbed a plate off the tray and presented it to her new stepmother. "It's chocolate. Daddy's favorite."

"Thank you." Lydia accepted the cake, wondering how on earth she'd ever be able to eat it. She seriously doubted that she could swallow a bite. Any food that got past her throat just might come back up.

"Here's coffee." Ruthie set a tray of cups on the nicked and scarred table in front of the couch, then sat down in a huge wooden rocker directly across from Lydia.

Molly bent over, resting her elbows on the arms of Lydia's chair. The child stared. "We're having an Easter egg hunt at school next month, and all the mothers are invited."

"Molly." Wade eased his big body to the edge of the couch. Although he knew how starved his child was for a mother, he didn't want her putting any extra pressure on Lydia. If his marriage was to have any chance of succeeding, he'd have to take things slow and easy and make sure his family didn't create any problems.

"I'd love to go to your Easter egg hunt," Lydia said, her eyes stinging with tears, her heart touched by the child's eagerness. "I have a huge basket that was mine when I was a little girl. I'll have my brother send it to me."

"How big is it?" Molly asked, bending closer and closer to Lydia.

Stretching her hands apart vertically and then horizontally, Lydia measured off a basket of enormous proportions. "On Saturday night before Easter, we'll put the basket at the foot of your bed and see if the Easter Bunny pays you a visit."

Lydia watched as Molly's eyes grew wide with wonder and delight, and Lydia remembered all the years the Easter Bunny had visited her. She'd been nine years old before she'd found out that her father was the bunny who had filled her basket with goodies each year.

"The Easter Bunny's never come here to the farm before," Molly said. "Daddy always buys me one of those fixed-up baskets at the dollar store. We didn't know about putting an empty basket at the foot of my bed, did we, Grandma?"

"Well, daddies and old grandmas don't always know about stuff like Easter bunnies. But young mamas do." Ruthie picked up a cup from the tray and took a sip of her coffee. "Y'all finish up here. We want to get on over to the trailer and leave these newlyweds alone."

"The trailer?" Lydia asked.

"You and Molly are leaving?" Wade asked at the same moment Lydia spoke.

Ruthie turned to her new daughter-in-law. "Britt and Tanya live in a trailer about a quarter of a mile down the road. Me and Molly are gonna spend the night with them tonight and give you and Wade a little privacy. Lord knows you won't get much from now on."

"Mrs. Cameron, that isn't necessary." Lydia wasn't sure she wanted to be alone with her silent and sulky groom.

"Yes, it's necessary. And quit calling me Mrs. Cameron. You can call me Ruthie, and someday when you get to know me better and have a mind to, you can call me Ma."

"Thank you, Ruthie." Lydia felt a tremendous gratitude toward her mother-in-law. She knew that Wade's mother could have caused them a great deal of trouble if she'd chosen to.

"I'll get Molly off to school from over at the trailer, so you two sleep as late as you'd like." Ruthie set her coffee cup down, picked up a plate, took two bites of cake and set the plate back down. "Well, I'm ready to go." She stood up. "Molly, let's get our suitcase."

Molly, still leaning over Lydia's chair, reached out and touched the delicate pearl choker round Lydia's neck. "That's so pretty. You wear a lot of jewelry, don't you? I don't have any jewelry."

"We'll have to see about getting you a necklace," Lydia said.

"Britt, go warm up the truck." Ruthie pulled Molly to a standing position and led her out into the hall.

"I'll be expecting you down at the chicken house at the regular time in the morning," Britt told his brother, then headed for the front door.

When Tanya approached her, Lydia stood. "Don't let Britt's sour attitude bother you," Tanya said, giving Lydia a hug. "He's a good man with a good heart, he just can't get over the accident... Paul dying... and then marrying me and... Well, just don't judge him until you get to know him better."

Suddenly Lydia and Wade were left all alone. She looked over at him and tried to force a smile.

"I'll get your bags out of the truck." He moved past her, not pausing to touch her or even look at her. He stopped at the front door. "After I put your stuff in our room, I've got to go out. It won't take me long, but there are a few things around this farm that won't wait.''

When she didn't reply, he made a hasty departure. Within minutes he returned with her bags, then went upstairs without saying a word. Before Lydia had a chance to do more than look around the living room, Wade came back downstairs. He'd changed into his jeans and work shirt. He gave her a quick kiss on the cheek, then went outside, slamming the door behind him.

Lydia slipped the dishes, one by one, into the warm soapy water. She couldn't remember if she'd ever washed dishes by hand before tonight. When she was a girl, there had always been a housekeeper to take care of such mundane chores, then when she'd had her own apartment, a dishwasher had been standard kitchen equipment. Of course, her house in town had a dishwasher and a three-days-a-week maid.

Lydia looked down at her hands. Small, soapy bubbles sparkled off the shiny new ring she wore. The thick band of gold on Lydia's finger felt strange. That simple symbol of a lifetime commitment reminded her of what a farce her first marriage had been. Tyler had given her a two-carat diamond, but his vows to love, honor and be faithful had been worthless. Now she wondered what those same promises meant to her new husband.

Looking outside the large kitchen window, Lydia sought a glimpse of Wade, wishing he wouldn't take so long to "check on things" again. He'd been gone over two hours. Having taken that time to explore her new home, Lydia had found the old farmhouse sadly lacking. Although the basic structure seemed sound, and she suspected a Victorian beauty lay beneath all the numerous coats of paint and layers of atrocious wallpaper and cheap paneling, Wade's home looked as if it had been decorated in garage sale rejects. The house would have been an eyesore to anyone with an ounce of good taste, but to an interior designer, the place was a nightmare. She only hoped that she'd be able to persuade Wade and his mother to allow her to start renovations—and soon.

When Wade had finished checking on things the first time, he'd suggested they eat an early supper because he needed to go back out again. Before she could open her mouth to voice an opinion, he'd reminded her that she was now a farmer's wife and would have to get used to the fact that he had to work long, hard hours.

Ruthie had left fried chicken and biscuits in the oven, potato salad, stuffed eggs and tea in the refrigerator, and the remainder of the chocolate "wedding cake" on the counter. They had eaten in silence—Wade's appetite enormous, Lydia's practically nonexistent. He'd told her that if she intended to be a farm wife, she'd have to eat more because she'd need her strength. She had informed him that she might be living on a farm now, but she had no intention of being a housewife. When she'd reminded him that she was going to resume her career as an interior designer, he'd asked who she thought would hire her now that she was married to a redneck farmer. Then he'd downed the last bites of cake and iced tea, got up from the table and told her to make herself at home while he finished the evening chores.

Lydia washed their tea glasses first, then set them on the rack to dry while she tackled the silverware and dishes. Ruthie hadn't left any dirty pots and pans, and the kitchen, though terribly out of date and in need of numerous repairs, was spotlessly clean.

What if Wade was right? she wondered. What if the people who'd been so eager to hire Lydia Reid as their decorator, weren't interested in Mrs. Wade Cameron?

Even though Lydia had been well aware that the news of her pregnancy and subsequent marriage plans had become the talk of the town, no one, except Glenn and Eloise, had actually confronted her. Eloise had been livid. Glenn had suggested a doctor in Birmingham who could take care of her "little problem." When she'd made it perfectly clear to both Glenn and his mother that she intended to keep her child and marry its father, Eloise had taken great pains to inform Lydia that such a foolish action would ruin her socially. Glenn had proposed marriage, and when she rejected his offer, he'd wished her well, telling her that if she ever needed him, he'd be there for her.

During the days before her wedding, Lydia had waited for the mysterious caller to act, and he or she had . . . last night. She hadn't told Wade and probably wouldn't, unless . . . Surely, now that she was married to Wade Cameron, the caller would have no reason to continue making useless threats.

Lydia finished the dishes, made a mental note of what all needed to be done to the kitchen, then went upstairs to the bedroom where Wade had placed her luggage. She wasn't sure, but she assumed it was Wade's room, although, except for a few stuffed animals and toys in one room, this bedroom was indistinguishable from the other three. Wide-plank hardwood floors, twelve-foot ceilings, faded, dollar-store drapes hanging at all the long, narrow windows, battered old furniture and an assortment of brightly colored throw rugs gave each upstairs room an almost identical appearance.

Lydia breathed a sigh of relief when she discovered a small bathroom adjacent to *their* bedroom. Needless to say, the fixtures were archaic, but she adored the claw-foot tub. Several clean towels lay on the back of the commode along with an unwrapped bar of soap and two washcloths. Ruthie's work, no doubt. Lydia smiled at the thought of a long, hot soak in this antique bathtub. At the rate things were going, it was likely to be the highlight of her wedding night.

After checking the closet, dresser and chest, Lydia found that no room had been made for her possessions. She'd just have to leave everything packed until morning . . . everything except her blue gown, robe and slippers.

This had been the longest and most difficult day of her life, and she longed for it to come to an end. Wade hadn't even tried to make things easier for her. Ever since his family had left, in order to give them some privacy, he had found endless chores to keep him away from her. Well, she had no intention of waiting downstairs until he decided to end his work day. She'd take a bath and go to bed, and if she were lucky she'd be asleep by the time he came upstairs.

Wade eased open the back door, stepped inside the dark kitchen and listened for any sounds of Lydia moving about downstairs. He heard the hum of the hot water heater, the crackling from the wood stove in the living room and the ticktock of Ma's mantel clock. Just the usual harmony of nighttime quiet within the old farmhouse.

Without a doubt this had been the longest day of Wade's life. He had a new wife and a second child on the way, but he had no idea how he was going to cope with either the financial or the emotional burden. He was in debt way over his head. It took every penny he and Britt could scrape together to keep the place going and provide the bare essentials for Molly and Ma and Tanya. How was he going to support two more people?

He knew Lydia had the means to take care of herself and their child better than he could, but he didn't want her to have to spend her own money or any of the money Tyler Reid had left her. Hell, a man took care of his own, and that definitely included a new wife and baby.

He was well aware of the fact that Lydia hadn't really wanted to marry him, that she dreaded living on the farm and hated giving up her comfortable home in town. But she'd agreed to the marriage for the same reason he'd proposed—for the sake of their unborn child.

He had wanted Lydia Reid to the point of madness. And he'd taken her without any thought of the consequences. Now they'd both have to pay for that night of passion.

Wade climbed the stairs, dreading the moment he'd have to face Lydia. He'd acted like a coward today, leaving her alone, going on with his chores as if it hadn't been his wedding day. She'd deserved better treatment from him, a little more consideration, but he'd been afraid to be alone with her. Despite the fact that a certain amount of distrust and wariness existed between them, Wade still wanted her, but he wasn't sure she felt the same way.

He would have liked nothing better than to have taken her to bed and spent the whole evening making love to her. While he'd been down at the chicken houses and out at the barn, he'd thought about Lydia. About the sweetness of her scent. About her soft skin and silky hair. For hours his body had been primed and ready to mate.

The door to his bedroom stood open, and only the faint moonlight filtering through the thin drapes illuminated the old brass bed where Lydia lay. Quietly moving into the room, he slipped by the bed, then stopped to take a look at the woman who seemed to be sleeping peacefully. She'd pulled the covers up to her neck so all he could see was her face and her golden brown hair spread out over the white pillowcase.

Opening the door to the bathroom, he flipped on the light and left the door ajar. Taking his time, he undressed, piling his clothes in a heap on the bathroom floor and propping his boots against the wall. He stepped inside the bathtub, drew the vinyl shower curtain and turned on the leaky shower.

When she heard the shower running, Lydia opened her eyes and glanced toward the bathroom. She looked at the old alarm clock on the wooden stand beside the bed. It was only nine o'clock. When he came to bed, would he realize she really wasn't asleep? Would he talk to her? Try to help her adjust to her new life? Would he expect them to make love?

Tossing and turning, Lydia counted the minutes, her heart hammering loudly, while she waited for her new husband to emerge from the bathroom. Although she dreaded the confrontation, a part of her longed for him to take her into his arms and promise her that everything would be all right.

Fifteen minutes later Wade Cameron, as naked as the day he was born, came out of the bathroom. His damp black hair glistened in the moonlight.

Lydia swallowed, then closed her eyes and lay perfectly still while Wade crawled into bed beside her. She could hear the roar of her own heartbeat as it drummed in her ears, and she felt certain that Wade could hear it, too.

"I know you're awake," he said, turning over in the bed so that he faced her.

She forced herself to remain calm, not to panic, then moved as far away from him as possible. "Did you finish your chores?"

"For today. They'll start all over again at five in the morning." He eased closer to her, his knee bumping against her leg.

Lydia tensed at the feel of his body touching hers. "I suppose you'll want me to get up and fix your breakfast."

"Since Ma won't be here, it'd be nice if you would, but I don't expect you to. I don't imagine you're used to getting up so early."

"I'm not much of a cook, but I can fix you an omelet."

He reached out and pulled her into his arms. Her silky gown rubbed against him where it covered her from breasts to knees. "Take off your gown."

"What?" She tried to pull out of his embrace, but he tightened his hold.

"This is our wedding night. We're man and wife. One of the advantages of marriage is being able to sleep together." Running his hand down the side of her body, he grabbed the hem of her gown, lifting it to her hips. "Take it off."

"I can't take it off with you holding me so tight," she said.

He released her, then scooted up in the bed, propping his elbow on his pillow. Slowly, hesitantly, Lydia pulled the gown up and over her head. Wade reached out, grabbed the silky garment and tossed it onto the floor. When he pulled her into his arms again, she went rigid for a moment, then began to tremble.

"I'm not going to hurt you." Wade realized she was frightened, and the thought displeased him greatly. He had never hurt a woman in his life. Why should his own wife be afraid of him?

"I know. It's just...just..." She choked on her tears, her body shaking with the repressed sobs.

Running one hand down her back, he soothed her, petting her gently. With his other hand, he brushed the tears from her cheeks. "I want you, Lydia. I want to hold you and kiss you and make love to you. You're my wife now, and I'm going to try to make this marriage work, for all our sakes."

"I...I want our marriage to succeed, too." She relaxed against him, her body already remembering the pleasure it had received from this man. "I just wasn't expecting my life to turn out this way. I'm not prepared to live out here on the farm, to be a mother to Molly, to be a wife to you."

"We'll take it one day at a time." Wade kissed her forehead, then her cheeks and chin. "It's not going to be easy for any of us."

"Oh, Wade, I'm so sorry." She flung her arms around him, hugging him to her, lavishing tiny kisses over his shoulder. "I know this isn't what you wanted, either."

He encircled her throat with his big hand, tilting her chin with his thumb. Looking down into her moist eyes, he smiled. "I might not have planned on marrying again, but don't ever think I don't want you." Grabbing her hip with his other hand, he pulled her closer, his thrusting arousal hard and hot against her.

Lydia sighed, surrendering herself to the feelings growing steadily within her. "Sex isn't going to be enough," she said just as he lowered his head.

With his lips brushing against hers, he whispered, "Maybe not, but for now it's all we've got." He covered her mouth with his own, letting his hand move down to take one breast while he massaged her buttocks, clutching, patting, rubbing.

He wanted this woman, wanted her more than he'd ever wanted anything in his life, but he couldn't let himself love her. He didn't dare put his fate in her hands. Because of Macie, he doubted he'd ever be able to completely trust another woman. He'd give Lydia what he was capable of giving her, and take whatever she could give in return.

Grabbing the sheet and quilts, Wade flung the covering toward the foot of the bed, leaving himself and Lydia lying naked and exposed to each other. "I want to look at you," he said, sitting up, running his hand down the front of her body from breasts to thighs and back up again. "I love to look at you. At your breasts. At those pretty pink nipples." He leaned over, took a puckered nipple into his mouth and sucked greedily.

Lydia moaned when she felt the instant tug inside her, that sensual connection between her breasts and the center of her feminine body. "Wade..."

He slipped his hand between her thighs, easing them slightly apart. With slow, repetitive strokes he rubbed his thumb against her taut flesh while he penetrated her with his fingers. She arched her back off the bed and cried out.

Lifting one leg over her, Wade settled himself on top of her, bracing himself with his big hands placed on each side of her body.

"Look at me," he said when she closed her eyes and sighed. "I want to watch you. I want to see you melt."

She threw her arms around him, pulling him down to her. "Please, Wade...please." She wanted to tell him that she loved him, that she could offer him more than just the pleasures of sex, but she didn't dare risk letting him know the extent of the power he held over her. She'd given Tyler Reid her heart, had entrusted her whole life to him, and he had betrayed her. At least in this marriage, she knew from the beginning that her husband didn't love her. But she had every intention of changing that situation. Somehow she'd find a way to make Wade Cameron love her.

She could feel his arousal, strong and demanding, as he poised above her, his manhood touching the soft curls between her thighs. Arching her hips higher, she issued a silent invitation.

"Tell me, Lydia. Tell me." He licked one hardened nipple, then ran his tongue across one breast to the other, taking that nipple into his mouth, flicking back and forth.

"I want you." She ran her hands down his back to his firm buttocks, then grabbed his tight flesh, beckoning him, pleading for his possession. If all they had was sex, then she'd use it to her advantage.

He surged into her with one powerful push, joining their bodies for a mating dance as old as time and as powerful as any of nature's elemental forces. He drove into her again and again, each stab quicker and harder, more demanding than the preceding one. Lydia responded, her own body tightening and releasing, preparing for the moment it would reach the pinnacle.

While his manhood dominated her femininity, his mouth conquered hers with thrusting kisses that left them both breathless and longing for more. He took her hips in his big hands, lifting her, positioning her for those last wild lunges that drove them both over the edge and into the abyss of earth-shattering pleasure.

She quivered with release, crying out, her nails biting into his buttocks as he gave himself over to the finality of the moment, his body shaking with fulfillment.

He eased off her, pulling her into his arms as he lay down beside her. Neither of them spoke, but they could hear each other's labored breaths and pounding hearts.

Hours later, while Lydia lay sleeping, Wade stood at the windows looking out over the backyard and vast acres that comprised his farm. Occasionally he glanced over at the bed, at the woman who was now his wife. Lydia was totally unsuited to life on the farm. She was well educated and cultured—a town woman, a lady who'd spent her entire life in the lap of luxury.

He couldn't help but wonder how long she'd be able to tough it out, how long she'd be willing to work at making their marriage work. He knew it was just a matter of time before she'd leave. And even though he had no intention of letting her departure break his heart, he did intend to make the most of the days, and especially the nights, they would have together. If sex was all they had, then he'd use it to his advantage.

Nine

Lydia held the telephone to her ear, listening as the caller warned her to leave her husband, that if she remained on the farm, she would regret it. Her hand trembled as she hung up the receiver. Today's call made the fifth—one a week—since her marriage to Wade last month.

Although the calls unnerved her terribly, Lydia hadn't told anyone else about the continued harassment. The mysterious caller had taken no action against her or anyone in the Cameron family, so Lydia decided that it was better not to tell Wade. After all, things between them were difficult enough as it was, without adding to their problems. The tension between Wade and her had increased steadily, both of them trapped in a marriage neither had wanted. A marriage for which neither of them had been prepared. So, as long as the caller didn't put his words into action, Lydia felt certain she could deal with the hollow threats.

"Is that Tanya?" Ruthie Cameron called from the kitchen.

"No, it was a wrong number." Lydia leaned back against the wall, taking several deep breaths.

"We've been getting quite a few of those," Ruthie said.

"Have the eggs finished boiling?" Lydia asked.

"Almost," Molly said. "I'm stirring the dye just like you showed me. I think it's ready."

"I'll be there in just a minute." Lydia squared her shoulders, straightened the turtleneck collar on her pullover and walked to the front door, which stood open, allowing the April sunshine to flood the hallway.

Fresh and young and new. The world outside wore springtime garments in various shades of green and pastel hues of pink and yellow. Tomorrow would be Easter Sunday, a day to celebrate the renewal of life.

Lydia dropped her hand to her stomach. The new life growing inside of her had made subtle changes in her body, but only the most discerning eye could detect that Lydia Cameron was over three months pregnant. Indeed, sometimes, Lydia found it hard to believe that she carried Wade's child. Ruthie had told her that she was one of those lucky women who wasn't bothered by daily bouts of morning sickness or plagued by listlessness and moody behavior.

It was a good thing that she hadn't been overly emotional the last few weeks or she would have either killed Wade or left him. Although alone at night in their bedroom, Wade was a loving husband who catered to her every sexual desire, bringing her to heights of pleasure she'd never known, he acted like a polite stranger during the day. In the darkness he touched her with passion and whispered steamy words and phrases that made her tremble with desire. In the daylight he treated her with respect, but kept her at arm's length.

And they argued about everything. He didn't want her to work. She'd told him that she gave up her career for Tyler, but she didn't intend to make the same mistake twice. She had completed one project and had taken on two new clients. Although her pregnancy and marriage to Wade continued to be the talk of the town, neither seemed to have affected people's opinion of her as a decorator. Of course, neither of her new clients was from Riverton. One lived in Tupelo and the other in Iuka.

Lydia wanted to start making some small changes in the farmhouse, but she hadn't dared approach Wade on the subject. Instead she'd talked to Ruthie, who'd thought it was a wonderful idea, but had warned her to tread lightly on Wade's masculine pride.

When she'd married Wade, she'd worried about winning over his old-fashioned, countrified mother and had wondered how Molly would react to having a new woman in the house—and, in a few months, a baby.

Ruthie Cameron was open and honest. She'd told Lydia that she and Wade were poorly suited and would have "a hard way to go" to make their marriage work, but that love could unite them if they had the courage to trust each other. Strange, that Wade's mother understood the biggest hurdle both she and Wade would have to overcome was the pain and anger left over from their previous marriages. They both found it difficult to trust again, to freely give their hearts to another. They were too afraid and too insecure. Not once had Wade said he loved her, and she couldn't bring herself to tell him.

Molly had been so starved for a mother that she had accepted Lydia without reservation and actually took Lydia's side over her father's whenever the two dared to disagree in front of the child. And when they'd told her about the baby, she'd seemed genuinely thrilled at the prospect of becoming a big sister.

Lydia had called her mother in Houston to tell her about her marriage. Joan's negative reaction hadn't surprised her. But, true to form, Joan had sent them a wedding present— a silver coffee service.

Lydia had told her brother in person, and he'd taken the news better than she'd expected. He'd even rummaged around in the attic of his home, the house in which the two of them had grown up, to find Lydia's old Easter basket.

Molly had loved the huge wicker basket and had carried it proudly to the school Easter egg hunt yesterday. Lydia had helped her dye eggs and prepare the basket Thursday night, then had joined the other mothers for lunch at school on Friday before the party. Child and stepmother had been the focus of everyone's attention. Lydia was grateful that Molly hadn't noticed the women's stares and whispers. She'd been so happy that she'd had a mother in attendance, for the first time in her life, just like everybody else.

"Grandma says the eggs are ready." Molly came up beside Lydia and tugged on her hand.

"Good. We want to get everything set up for tomorrow." Lydia grasped the child's hand and maneuvered her down the hallway and back into the kitchen.

"Do you really think the Easter Bunny will visit the farm tonight?" Molly asked.

Lydia caught a glimpse of Ruthie as she poured cake batter into greased pans. The two exchanged knowing smiles. "I guarantee it. All we have to do is place your basket at the foot of your bed." Quickly Lydia calculated all the items she had hidden in the top of her closet—items the Easter Bunny would deliver late tonight after Molly was asleep.

"You two better hurry up and get those eggs dyed if you want to show them to Wade. He'll be coming in for lunch in less than an hour." Ruthie opened the oven door, pulled out the rack and arranged the three cake pans in a triangle.

Lydia drained the water from the pan, then scooped the eggs out, one by one, placing them in the individual bowls of food coloring. "Take a spoon and keep turning the eggs around and around."

Molly went from bowl to bowl, rotating the eggs. "Grandma, me and Lydia are going to fix up my room. Lydia says it'll be a birthday present from her and Daddy. And she's moving her doll collection from her house in town to put in my room."

Ruthie arched one bushy gray brow. "Well, that'll be some fine present, won't it?"

"I thought Molly's room would be the perfect place to start doing a little redecorating." Lydia searched her mother-in-law's eyes for a sign of approval.

"Well, since Molly's birthday is in June, you should have plenty of time. That'll leave you nearly four months to fix Britt's old room up into a nursery for Molly's little brother." Ruthie ran her fingers through Molly's black curls, ruffling the child's hair in a playful manner.

"How can the doctor tell that our baby is a boy?" Molly continued turning the eggs in the dye solution.

The sound of dogs barking preceded the loud knocks outside the house. Lydia opened the kitchen door and looked toward the front porch. Glenn Haraway stood just outside the screen door.

"They got tests they run on mamas, now," Ruthie said. "Who is it?" she asked Lydia.

"It's Glenn Haraway."

"Why am I not surprised?" Ruthie wiped her hands off on her apron. "You want me to ask him in or—"

"No, I'll go." Lydia turned to Molly. "Take the eggs out and set them in the tray to dry."

Lydia was glad to see Glenn. Even though he'd called to check on her several times in the past few weeks and she'd spoken with him and Eloise at Sunday church services, this was Glenn's first visit to the farm since her marriage.

Lydia opened the screen door. "Come on in, Glenn. Is this a social call?"

He stepped into the hall, looked around, then focused his gaze on Lydia. "Well, yes and no. I've been meaning to get out this way to see you, but I wasn't too sure how your new husband would feel about it."

"Wade knows that we've been friends for years."

"Hmmm. Well, I need to discuss a little business with Mrs. Cameron, then maybe you and I can take a walk and you can show me the farm."

"What business do you have with Ruthie?"

"Time has just about run out." Glenn ran a slender finger around the neck of his button-down shirt, loosening his tie just a bit. "She's got to sell her land down on Cotton Row, or Riverton can kiss that new mall goodbye."

"She isn't going to sell. She has a blind spot where those old buildings are concerned."

"I wish a tornado would level that old gin, then maybe she'd sell." Glenn put his arm around Lydia's shoulder. "Look, Lydia, since you're a member of the family now, you should be trying to persuade her. After all, the Camerons need money badly. Those boys are up to their eyeballs in debt trying to pay off some old loans and keep up payments on the loan that paid for those new chicken houses."

"Everybody in town knows how I feel about preserving those buildings on Cotton Row. My grandpa and his afore him ran that gin," Ruthie said as she walked down the hall, Molly following directly behind her. "My pa didn't have nothing, not a dime to his name when he died, but he left me that land. It's all I got from him, and I don't aim to sell it so some rich folks can get richer."

"But Mrs. Cameron—" Glenn dropped his arm from around Lydia.

"Molly finished up those eggs," Ruthie said. "She wants to show her daddy her new Easter outfit when he comes in for lunch."

Lydia checked the time on her wristwatch. "Your daddy should be home soon. Do you want me to go up with you and help you change?"

"No need for that," Ruthie said, taking Molly by the hand. "You stay here and entertain your guest, and I'll go up and help Molly put on all that new stuff you bought her."

"I bet when Daddy sees how pretty I look, he'll go to church with us tomorrow." Molly smiled at Lydia, then followed her grandmother upstairs.

"Buying clothes for Cameron's daughter?" Glenn asked. "If they'd sell the Cotton Row land, he'd have enough money to pay for her clothes himself."

"Wade provides well for his child." Lydia's face flushed pink. She didn't like to hear Glenn condemning her husband. "But she's my child now, too, and I enjoy buying things for her."

"Are you enjoying playing wifey and mother out here on the farm?" Glenn laughed, his gaze narrowing as he eyed Lydia. "You aren't cut out for the rural life. You're going to get bored living in a run-down farmhouse, breathing in the smell of cattle and chickens, having no one to talk to every day but a bunch of hicks."

"Glenn, you're being offensive." Lydia balled her hands into fists, surprised by how much she wanted to strike her old friend. "The Camerons are fine people. I'm very fond of them."

"Look, Lydia, why don't you admit that you made a mistake. You let Cameron take advantage of you and then railroad you into marriage." Glenn took Lydia's hands and brought them to his lips, kissing them tenderly. "You should have had an abortion, and no one would have been the wiser."

Lydia pulled on her hands, but Glenn held her tightly. "I love this child. I could never . . . never . . ."

"You're going to get tired of living like this." Glenn gestured toward the dismal interior of the house. "Cameron's an uncouth redneck without a dime to his name."

"Glenn if you're going to continue to speak about my husband like that, I'm going to have to ask you to leave." Lydia jerked her hands free, but Glenn put his arm around her shoulder and pulled her close to his side.

"I'll be waiting for you when you come to your senses." Glenn hugged her, and when she tried to shove him away, he tightened his hold. "I'll even take the child. After all, it will be yours, and that's what matters."

Wade Cameron stormed into the hall from the kitchen. His long legs covered the short distance in a split second. Lydia cringed at the sight of him. He glared at her and Glenn, then pulled her out of Glenn's arms and grabbed him by the throat.

"What matters is that the child she's carrying is mine!" Wade shoved Glenn up against the wall, clutching him in a stranglehold.

"Wade, please don't." Lydia rushed over to the two men and tugged on Wade's rock-hard arm.

"I'd like nothing better than to knock some sense into you." Wade lowered his head to within inches of the shorter man's, squinted his eyes and smiled. "But if I wipe the floor with you, Lydia will be upset, and I don't want my pregnant wife to get upset."

"Wade..." Lydia stepped away from the two men, praying silently that her husband would retain control of his temper.

Just at that moment Molly Cameron came bouncing down the stairs dressed in pink ruffles and bows. Lydia rushed over to the bottom of the stairs, hoping to divert her attention from her father.

"What's the matter?" Molly asked. "Are Daddy and that man fighting?"

"No." Lydia took Molly's hand and tried to turn her around.

Ruthie came down the steps slowly, carefully placing one foot in front of the other as she held on to the banisters. "Molly, you come on back up here."

"But Grandma, Daddy and that man—"

"Molly Cameron!" Ruthie motioned to her granddaughter, who instantly ran back up the stairs.

Wade grasped Glenn Haraway by the back of the neck, whirled him around and walked him to the front door. He kicked the screen door open and marched his wife's guest outside, giving him a hard shove off the porch. Glenn staggered, then fell to the ground. Quickly he picked himself up, dusted off his suit and jumped into his Audi.

"You're not welcome here, Mr. Haraway," Wade shouted. "And stay away from my wife, or the next time I won't act like a gentleman."

Lydia felt her body begin to tremble; a slow, steady quivering from her fingers to her toes. Wade came back inside, slamming the front door. He grabbed her by the shoulders.

"Stay away from Haraway. You're my wife now, and I won't have you spending time with another man."

"I think you have me confused with your first wife."

Ignoring her comment, Wade pulled her closer and looked deeply into her eyes. "That man is in love with you. He wants you. He hates me because I've had what he wants."

Salty bile rose in her throat, threatening to choke her. "Glenn . . . Glenn came here to see your mother, to talk to her about selling the Cotton Row property."

"That was as good an excuse as any, I suppose." Wade threaded his fingers through her hair, grasping the back of her head while he held her securely by one shoulder.

"It's the truth."

"Is it?"

"I don't lie."

"Don't you?"

She tried to free herself from his tenacious hold, but he refused to release her. "Nothing happened. You're acting as if—"

"I walk into my home and find a man telling my wife that he'll be waiting for her when she comes to her senses and leaves me." He lowered his head until his lips touched hers. "He wants you so bad, he'd be willing to take my son if he could get you."

"Oh, Wade . . ."

His lips took hers with savage possession. He plunged his tongue into her mouth while he held her head in a viselike grip. When he finally released her, they were both breathing hard and fast, their pulses racing.

Lydia turned away from him. Wade circled her wrist with his big hand. "You're mine." He pulled her hand upward, shoving her fingers in front of her face. "This wedding band makes you mine." He brought her hand down to her stomach. "And this is mine."

She choked back the sobs in her throat, but tears escaped her eyes. "If I'm yours, then you should be mine. But I don't feel that you belong to me. Ever since we've been married, you've done nothing to make me feel loved and wanted."

She ran up the stairs, the tears blurring her vision, ignoring Ruthie Cameron who stood in the upstairs hallway.

Wade turned around and kicked the table on which the telephone sat. The force of his blow broke two of the rickety pine legs. The table crumpled. The telephone slid off onto the wooden floor with a thud. A tiny tinkling sound echoed in the deadly quiet.

"Damn!" Wade stomped back into the kitchen, cursing himself for being such a fool.

Wearing nothing but a towel draped around his hips, Wade lay across the bed, his arms crossed behind his head as he watched Lydia stand on tiptoe to reach the shelf in their closet.

"Need some help?" he asked, rising up off the bed.

"No, thank you." She pulled down a large paper bag.

Wade was surprised she'd answered him at all. She hadn't spoken a single word to him since he'd lost his temper with her earlier that day. Of course, he didn't blame her. He had acted like a jealous idiot. He didn't regret anything he'd said or done to Glenn Haraway, but he wished he could take back the hurtful accusations he'd hurled at his wife.

When Lydia opened the bedroom door, Wade called out to her. "Are you sure Molly's asleep?"

"Yes. I checked on her a few minutes ago." Lydia stepped out into the hall.

Wade walked over to the door and watched Lydia ease into Molly's room. His wife was playing Easter Bunny for his daughter. He'd never seen Molly so excited as she'd been the past few days, planning for Lydia's visit to the school Easter egg hunt, waiting for the Easter Bunny's first visit to the farm, ecstatic over her first store-bought Easter outfit.

Damn, Lydia had been more of a mother to Molly in a few weeks than Macie had been in six years. And, he admitted to himself, if he'd just give her half a chance, she'd be more of a wife to him.

He didn't know how to say he was sorry. He didn't know the right words to use with a woman like Lydia. The only common ground they seemed to share was in bed, with the lights low and the day left far behind. Perhaps he could apologize by making love to her. If sex was all they had, then he'd have to make good use of it.

Wade stripped naked, threw back the covers and lay down. He reached out to turn off the lamp on his side of the bed. The lamp on Lydia's side gave a minimum of light, casting gray shadows over the room.

Lydia hesitated outside the bedroom, wanting to talk to Wade and yet dreading another confrontation. If only he'd meet her halfway, they might have a chance of making their marriage work. She wanted to be Wade's wife, in every way possible. She loved him, the big, stubborn redneck! All she wanted was for him to love her in return.

She slipped off her robe and laid it at the foot of the bed, then lay down beside her naked husband. She knew he was aroused and probably would make love to her. The thought excited her, but she didn't know if they could ever solve their problems this way. There had to be more between them than sex or they would keep repeating the same mistakes over and over again. She wanted an apology from her husband. Two simple words—I'm sorry.

The moment she lay down beside him, he reached for her, pulling her close, nuzzling her ear. She lay rigid in his arms, willing herself not to respond, when already her heart beat wildly and her body softened at his touch.

"I want you," he whispered, moving his hands up and under her gown.

When she didn't reply, he leaned over, taking her mouth in a hungry, forceful kiss. She didn't fight him, but she willed herself not to participate. Within minutes he realized that she wasn't responding.

"Are you punishing me?" he asked, closing one big hand over her breast, squeezing tightly.

She swallowed back the words she wanted to say, trying desperately not to cry.

"You're my wife. I want you." He slid his hand between her closed thighs and dipped his fingers inside her warmth. "And you want me, dammit. You're hot and wet."

She couldn't deny that she wanted him. All he had to do was touch her and she melted with need, and he knew from the physical evidence that he could take her, that she could deny him nothing. But she wouldn't give him the satisfaction of admitting it to him. If there was ever going to be more than sex between them, Wade Cameron would have to learn that his wife, his new wife, wanted his love and respect.

He covered one breast with his mouth, his tongue drawing moist circles through the thin silk material of her gown. Her body quivered. She moaned. Wade shoved her gown up to her waist, then moved atop her, parting her legs with his knee. When he entered her, she reached out, clinging to his shoulders as he smothered her face with wet, wild kisses.

Their bodies mated with the frenzy of desire and anger, passion and despair. Fast and hard, he moved in and out, taking her higher and higher, his whole masculine being acting in a primeval rage while his mate succumbed to him and at the same time conquered him as surely as he did her.

Lydia smothered her cries of pleasure by burying her face against his arm and biting down into his muscled flesh. The intimate quivers inside her triggered his own release as he surged into her one final time, his body shuddering as he fell to her side, dragging her up against him.

Neither of them spoke as they lay there listening to the silence in the room. Only their own labored breathing echoed in their ears. Lydia pulled away, turning her back on him. When he touched her on the shoulder, she moved farther away from him.

"After that, you're still angry with me?" He couldn't believe that she didn't understand how much making love to her tonight had meant to him . . . how much it always meant to him.

"You said some terrible things to me." She looked toward the windows facing the backyard. "You upset Molly. You acted like an animal with Glenn."

"If you're so angry with me, why the hell did you let me make love to you?" He sat up in bed, grabbed her by the shoulder and turned her over to face him.

"You hardly gave me a choice." Tears streamed down her face. She swiped them away with the back of her hand.

"Are you saying that I forced you?" He glared at her, his eyes black as the night sky outside.

She couldn't control the sobs racking her body. "No . . . Wade . . . I . . ."

He jumped out of the bed, reached down, picked up his jeans and jerked them on. "If you don't want me to touch you, all you have to do is say so." He zipped his jeans. "I'll go sleep in Britt's old room tonight . . . and from now on, if that's what you want."

He hesitated when he reached the door. "When you decide you want me to make love to you again, you'll have to beg me."

"Wade—"

"You know where I'll be if you want me."

Ten

"Thank you for calling, Glenn. Please tell Eloise I'll stop by next time I'm in town. Bye." Lydia replaced the receiver on the old black telephone, which now sat on an overturned nail keg.

As she walked down the hall, she pulled her hair up into a ponytail and secured it with a rubber band she held in her hand. She picked up a straw hat lying on the kitchen table and put it on her head before going outside. She caught a glimpse of her mother-in-law squatted between two rows of tomato plants.

If a year ago anyone had told her that she'd be married to Wade Cameron, five months pregnant with his son and helping Ruthie make a vegetable garden, Lydia would have laughed in their face. But she wasn't laughing today, only a few weeks after the anniversary of Tyler's and Macie's deaths. No one in the Cameron household had mentioned it, not even Britt when he stopped by for coffee every morning while Wade finished his breakfast.

The afternoon sun warmed Lydia as she turned her face upward, looking out over the cloudless blue sky. She couldn't believe how much she'd grown to love the farm, the rich earth, the endless acres of plowed fields, the open space that seemed to go on forever.

During the past month, her life had settled into a routine. She got up at five and went downstairs to help Ruthie with breakfast. Her mother-in-law had taught her how to make biscuits. During the morning hours she used the dining room as her office. Wade had even added a longer cord to the telephone so she could set it on the table beside her and phone clients and wholesalers without getting up.

Except that he voiced no objections to her work, Wade's attitude toward her had changed very little. He was cordial and polite, always inquiring about how she felt and if she needed anything. But he never touched her, and he hadn't slept with her since the night he'd moved into Britt's old room. She missed sleeping with him. Not just the sex, which she craved, but the closeness of lying beside him through the night, of being able to reach out and touch him whenever she needed reassurance.

It had become obvious that he had no intention of swallowing his pride. She knew that the only way Wade would come back to her bed was if she begged him to, and her own pride wouldn't allow her to surrender. After all, he was the one who should be begging her forgiveness.

When Lydia joined Ruthie in the garden, the older woman stood up, wiping the sweat from her face with her hand.

"I think you're making a mistake staying friends with Glenn Haraway," Ruthie said. "If Wade finds out, he's liable to bust a gut."

"Glenn has apologized for what happened, and that's more than I can say for your son." Lydia glanced over the rows of seedlings just peeping through the earth, then at the taller plants that had taken growing spurts since yesterday's rain.

"It's not good for you two to be sleeping apart." Ruthie rubbed the small of her back, grunting as she massaged her fleshy waist. "Sex is what brought you two together. It's what can keep you together until love has a chance to grow."

Lydia's face flushed scarlet at the frankness of her mother-in-law's words. "Don't ever change, Ruthie. The world would be a better place if everyone was like you."

"How's that?"

"There wouldn't be any lies. Everyone would just tell the truth."

"Lying takes more brain power than I've got." Ruthie laughed, then suddenly frowned. "You're an honest woman yourself, Lydia. Wade hasn't gotten used to that, yet. He spent over six years with a woman who'd rather lie than eat when she was hungry."

Checking her watch, Lydia said, "It's almost time for the bus. I'd better go meet Molly."

Ruthie took Lydia by the arm. "I just heard Wade's truck drive up. You go on up to the house and fix him some iced tea. I'll meet Molly. I've been promising her that we'd go check in Waldrep's Woods to see if the blackberries are ready to pick."

"Giving Wade and me time alone won't solve our problems."

"Tell him that you're tired of sleeping alone and see what happens." Ruthie gave Lydia a gentle shove. "Go on. Get in that house and talk to your husband."

As soon as she poured two glasses of iced tea, Lydia walked out into the hall. Before she took two steps, she heard Wade's voice and then Britt's coming from the living room.

"I've talked to Tanya about our selling the trailer and moving back in here until things get better," Britt said. "But she didn't like the idea. She said that once Lydia's baby comes, there won't be room for all of us."

"There's no need for you to sell your trailer," Wade told his brother. "If nothing happens to the soybean crop and we can get top dollar on our beef, then we should break even this year."

"At least the chicken houses are paying for themselves, but without some extra money we can't make any improvements. The farm is going downhill fast."

"You don't have to tell me. And this house is falling in around us," Wade said.

"Your new wife is wanting to do some redecorating. Tanya says that Lydia has offered to use her own money." Britt grunted, slapped his brother on the back and laughed. "We know how to pick 'em, don't we, big brother? I married a woman who's still in love with her first husband, and you married a woman who—"

"Lydia doesn't love Tyler Reid."

"Maybe not, but she sure as hell doesn't love you, does she?"

The tea glasses chilled Lydia's hands, but she didn't dare move to put them down. She didn't want Wade or Britt to know she was listening to their conversation. Hoping she could slip back into the kitchen, she turned, but not before Britt came stomping out of the living room.

"Hello and goodbye," he said. "He's all yours, if you want him." Britt slammed the screen door as he left.

Lydia forced herself to walk into the living room and hand Wade a glass of tea.

"Thanks." He glanced at her, but then looked back down at the stack of envelopes lying on the coffee table.

"Wade. I . . . I couldn't help overhearing part of your conversation with Britt." She clutched her tea glass as if it were a lifeline.

He looked up at her, frowning. "You got something you want to say?"

"I have money. More than enough."

"No!"

"But I'm your wife. This is my home now. It will be my son's home." Her hand trembled, sloshing the cold tea onto her fingers.

"I will not take your money."

"Then let Ruthie sell her land on Cotton Row." Lydia sat down on the couch and placed her glass on the coffee table by the stack of unpaid bills.

"Have you been trying to persuade Ma to sell?"

"I haven't said a word to her about it. She's mentioned it to me several times."

"She doesn't want to sell that land and see all those buildings torn down," Wade said. "She's mighty proud that her family once owned the gin, that a few generations back her folks were important around these parts."

"I understand all that, but Ruthie also realizes how much the money could help you and Britt."

Wade reached down, took Lydia by the shoulders and jerked her up off the couch. "Dammit, woman. Stay out of my business."

It was the first time he'd touched her in nearly a month. His big hands felt hard and hot. She quivered at the memory of how those hands had stroked her body.

Wade pulled her closer. She struggled to free herself. Bending over, he touched her forehead with his own. "If you want me so badly, why haven't you invited me back to our bed?"

"Because I want more from this marriage than sex. I want a partnership. I want kindness and consideration and respect." She took a deep breath, trying to resist the temptation of his lips so close to hers. "Your mother and daughter have made me feel more welcome in this house than you have. They've tried to make me feel like a real member of the family."

"You want everything your own way."

"I want to share my life with you, Wade."

When he pulled her closer to his big body, she felt his arousal.

"Share your body with me," he said.

She pushed against him, tears forming in her eyes. "Please let me go."

He released her immediately. "You know you're driving me crazy, don't you? You know that I'm lying up there every night in a cold sweat, I want you so bad."

She whirled around and ran out of the living room. Just as she entered the hall, her toe caught on the corner of a bright green throw rug. Realizing she was losing her balance, Lydia grasped at thin air, trying to find something to break her fall.

Wade saw what was happening and rushed toward her, but didn't make it to her in time to catch her. She fell over onto the bottom stairstep, cried out and clutched her stomach. Wade knelt down beside her, taking her face in his big hands. She reached out, touching his chest with her fingertips as if she were afraid to let her hands rest against him.

"Oh, God, Lydia, I'm sorry." He ran his hands over her face. "Are you hurt?"

"I'm all right." She touched his cheek. "When I stumbled, the baby kicked."

"You're not hurt? You cried out because the baby kicked you?" With relief spreading through his tense body, Wade laughed as he searched her face for the truth.

"A strong, powerful kick." Teardrops fell from Lydia's eyes.

"Are you sure you're all right?" He pulled her up and into his arms, holding her tightly as he stroked her waist and hips. He pressed his mouth into her hair, kissing the shiny softness. "Don't cry. Please, don't cry."

"I've missed you so much." She moved her hands over his back, upward and across his massive shoulders, kneading the hard muscles she found there.

"I've missed you, too." Methodically he covered every inch of her face and neck with light, tender kisses while he fondled her with delicate caresses. He moved his hands in slow, worshipful abandonment, skimming her slender neck, touching her shoulders and arms with gentleness, brushing his fingertips cautiously across her full, heavy breasts.

She stood motionless in his arms, savoring each blissful touch, wanting to reciprocate, but allowing him the time for his loving examination. Her body had changed in the last month, and she realized that he wanted to experience those changes, first-hand.

He traced the outline of the top button on her loose aqua-and-white-striped sundress, briefly hesitating before flipping it open. Her heart beat rapidly, her breasts moving up and down with each breath she took. Ever so slowly he eased the second button through its opening. She looked at him, her eyes bright with passion.

"I want to see you," he said, releasing the third and fourth buttons. "I need to see you."

"I've gotten so big."

Swiftly he finished unbuttoning the dress, pulling it away from her body, letting it hang loosely from her shoulders. "My child is growing inside of you. Don't you know how that makes me feel?" Placing his hand behind her back, he released the catch on her bra and eased it downward.

"How...how does it make you feel?" Her voice quavered, her body swayed.

"Your breasts are full." He slid the dress down her hips, taking her half slip with it, then pulled the bra down her arms. She stood there totally naked except for a pair of aqua panties. "It makes me want you desperately. It makes me want to hold you and love and protect you."

When she began unbuttoning his shirt, he stopped her and took it off himself. He reached out and placed one big hand on her stomach. "He's moving."

"Your son is very active." Lydia wondered how much longer she would be able to stand on legs that had suddenly turned to jelly.

Wade lifted her into his arms and carried her up the stairs, taking the steps two at a time. Once inside their bedroom, he laid her down on the bed, easing his big body down beside her. She traced the features of his face with her finger-tips, lingering on his mouth. He kissed her fingers, one by one.

"Oh, Wade."

"It won't hurt you or the baby if we make love, will it?" he asked, as he kissed the narrow space between her swollen breasts.

"According to everything that I've read about pregnancy, sex is relatively safe up until the very end. I've even read about an ancient belief that frequent sex makes for a strong, healthy baby."

They both laughed, each looking into the other's eyes, their hearts so full, their minds and bodies so in harmony.

Wade bent over her, resting his head gently on her stomach, rubbing his cheek back and forth against its taut smoothness. Pulling her panties downward, he kissed her belly, his big hands cupping each side. "My child."

Suddenly Lydia's stomach moved. She knew what was happening but wasn't sure Wade did.

"Lydia?"

"Yes."

"He's kicking."

"Yes, he is."

He kissed her stomach again, then eased himself up, slipping his arms around Lydia, pulling her close. Warm and inviting, her mouth beckoned him. He covered her lips with his own, dipping his tongue inside her to taste her sweetness. He guided his hands over her body in a quick, feverish search, delving inside her panties to find the luscious moisture hidden beneath her golden curls. She squirmed against his hand, her body arching upward, pleading for more.

"You're so hot and wet. So incredibly sweet." He replaced his hand with his mouth while he pulled her panties down her hips and tossed them on the floor. Using his tongue, he stroked rhythmically across the secret heart of her.

She moaned, then cried out when his mouth explored her femininity with wild abandon. "Wade...please...I can't bear it!"

"Don't ask me to stop. I want to love you. I need to love you." He had deprived them both of the pleasure they found in each other's bodies. Because of his macho pride, he had crushed Lydia's tender feelings and doomed them to weeks of celibacy. In loving her now, he wanted to show her how sorry he was for the way he'd treated her. He wanted to make amends for any pain he'd caused.

"Wade..." It was the last coherent word she uttered for quite a while.

Wade had his way. He loved her body until she reached an earth-shattering release.

He lay with his head nestled against her slightly protruding stomach, petting her tenderly with one big hand. "Lydia, you're very special to me. You know that, don't you?" He moved his head from her stomach to her breasts, flicking his tongue across one rigid nipple.

"Oh..." She felt a new awakening deep inside her. Even though he'd brought her so much pleasure, she longed for a more complete loving.

"I can't get enough of you, woman," he admitted, moving his lips upward to cover hers.

He enveloped her in his arms, holding her naked body close to him, savoring the feel of her warmth. He moved his mouth over hers and found her lips soft and sweet and yielding. She moaned when he deepened the kiss.

Her surrender coursed through his body like wildfire, igniting a raging blaze of desire inside him. When she rose up, throwing her arms around him, clinging to him, he eased her back down onto the bed, exploring her body with trembling hands.

"Did you happen to read anything about the best possible positions in which to make love when you're five months pregnant?" he asked.

"I think if you can remove your jeans, I can arrange a very appropriate position." She couldn't help smiling when she noticed the look of helplessness on his rugged face.

"I'm not sure I can manage such a big job without help," he said, guiding her hands to his zipper.

Lydia ran her index finger down the length of the zipper and slowly edged her way back up. He groaned and grabbed her hand. "You witch. You know you're driving me crazy."

"If I'm a witch, you'd better be careful. I could be casting a spell over you right now."

"You cast a spell over me a long time ago. The first time I saw you. I took one look at those golden green eyes and I was lost."

"I know the feeling," she whispered, tapping her fingers up and down the swell of his manhood.

"Lydia . . ." he warned.

"Hmmm?"

"I'll take off my jeans if you'll stop tormenting me."

She lay against him, the sound of his erratic heartbeat echoing in her ear, the smell of his warm masculinity enticing her to bold action. With unsteady fingers she released his zipper, slid her hand inside his jeans and stroked the swollen bulge beneath his cotton briefs.

"Lydia!" he covered her hand with his own.

"Please, Wade, show me how to give you the pleasure you gave me." Her voice grew low and timidly soft, yet undeniably seductive.

"Are you sure?"

"Yes. Please. I want to so much."

Wade closed his hand about hers as it circled his manhood, and slowly, lovingly, she learned to give back to her passionate lover the excitingly intimate satisfaction that he had given her.

When Lydia awoke several hours later, Wade lay beside her, propped up on his elbow, watching her. She smiled at him.

"What time is it?" she asked.

"Nearly four-thirty."

She jumped out of the bed. "Oh, my goodness. Molly...
Molly will—"

Wade grabbed her by the arm, pulling her back into the
bed. "Ma met the bus. Molly's had a snack and now she's
outside helping Ma in the garden."

"You've been downstairs? You've talked to Ruthie?"

"After you dozed off to sleep, I sneaked downstairs to
retrieve our clothes." He ran his fingers across her collar-
bone and laughed when she sucked in her breath. "Ma
caught me."

"Oh, no. She didn't." Lydia covered her face with her
hands, then peeked at him between her separated fingers.
"What did she say?"

"She told me that she'd met Molly's bus and had taken
her over to Waldrep's Woods to check on the blackberries.
She's keeping her busy in the garden until suppertime."
Wade drew circles over one of Lydia's breasts and then the
other, his fingertips just barely touching her. "That means,
Mrs. Cameron, that you and I have about an hour."

"I can't believe Britt hasn't been back up here demanding your presence down at the chicken houses."

"He has. Ma suggested he go home and spend some time
with his own wife, then she sent him away." Wade chuck-
led, remembering the look on Britt's face.

Lydia reached up and pulled his head down to hers. "If
we only have an hour, then we'd better get started."

"You have missed me, haven't you," he said, his lips
brushing hers.

"I want you to come back to our bed. I want you to hold
me and kiss me and make love to me every night. And...and
if you want me to beg you, I will."

"I'm the one who should be begging." He breathed the
words into her mouth as he fumbled with his zipper.

She licked a moist trail up the side of his shoulder and
neck. "Make love to me, Wade. Please."

He yanked off his jeans and briefs, tossed them onto the floor and lay down beside Lydia, lifting her into his arms. He set her on top of him, clutching her hips. "I want to please you."

He surged up and into her. She slumped forward, her heavy breasts swaying over him like tempting fruit begging to be tasted. He allowed her to set the pace, slow and easy in the beginning, then building, building, building into a steady rhythm as their bodies moved in perfect precision. In. Out. Up. Down. Slick and hot and all consuming.

He tormented her breasts with his tongue while he caressed her hips and whispered steamy love words, telling her how good she felt, how much he wanted her, what he wanted to do to her... forever.

She increased the tempo of her ride until her movements became frantic—hard and fast and uncontrollable. When she cried out, he thrust up and into her several times in quick succession, then shuddered, joining her in a mutual release that left them both lost in unbearable pleasure.

"I love you," Lydia whispered, her body resting atop his.

He stroked the damp tendrils of hair from her face, kissing the side of her forehead. He didn't know if she actually meant what she'd said or if the words were a result of their tumultuous lovemaking. Whatever the reason, he treasured the words as much as he treasured Lydia. "We're going to make this marriage work," he said. "I promise you."

Eleven

Lydia arranged seven candles on the enormous pink and white birthday cake while Tanya poured pink lemonade into pink plastic cups.

"We'd better hurry and not leave Ruthie out there with all of those children for too long or she'll have them working in the garden." Lydia dropped a book of matches into the pocket of her white slacks, then picked up a serving knife and the cake plate off the counter.

Tanya laughed. It was the first time today that Lydia had even seen her smile.

"Is there something you want to talk about?" Lydia asked, hoping her sister-in-law wouldn't think she was prying. "I'm not being nosy, but if you want to cry on my shoulder—"

"I'm leaving Britt." The words rushed out of Tanya like air from a popped balloon.

"What?" Lydia set the knife and cake back down on the counter.

"I was going to wait until after the party to tell you. I don't want to ruin this day for you and Molly. The kid's never had a birthday party before. She's never had visits from the Easter Bunny or a mother to read her bedtime stories or—"

"Talk to me." Lydia put her arm around Tanya's shoulders. In the few months since she'd been a member of the Cameron family, she'd grown to like her immature little sister-in-law and had always suspected that Tanya's marriage wasn't a happy one.

Tanya turned into Lydia's arms, tears streaming down her cheeks. "I...I haven't told Britt that I'm leaving. He'll try to stop me. He keeps saying that we can work things out. We can't."

"Are you sure?" Lydia asked.

"We've been trying for two years."

"I can hardly give you any advice, considering the fact that my first husband didn't know the meaning of the word fidelity, and Wade...well, Wade married me because of our baby."

"You love him, don't you?" Tanya asked as she pulled away, wiping her eyes and trying to smile.

"Yes. I know it doesn't make any sense. We're so ill-suited, and of course he doesn't love me. I think he's afraid to let himself love and trust another woman after what Macie did to him." Lydia tore a paper towel from the rack and handed it to Tanya.

Tanya blotted her tears and smeared makeup on the towel. "Thanks."

"Does Ruthie know?"

"No, but I don't think she'll be too surprised. She tried to persuade us not to marry, tried to convince us that I wasn't ready." Tanya threw up her arms in a gesture of defeat. "Boy, was she right. I was still in love with Paul when I married Britt. But Britt said he'd always loved me and that if...if..."

"You don't have to explain."

"I tried to kill myself after Paul died. About three months after he died. You know Britt was driving the car, and he felt guilty. Thought it was his fault."

"Wade told me that Britt was in the hospital for over two months."

"Look, don't say anything to Ruthie or Wade, will you? I just wanted you to know so you can help Wade with Britt after I'm gone." Tanya picked up the tray of pink cups.

"Is there anything I can do?"

"No." Tanya pushed the back door open with her hip. "Just help the family see Britt through this." Tanya carried the tray outside.

Lydia hesitated before picking up the cake again. For the past two weeks, she had begun to hope that her marriage had a chance. Ever since Wade had carried her upstairs and made love to her the day he'd felt their child move for the first time, he'd been sharing her bed every night. He had been making love to her every night.

She'd begun to feel close to Wade, to trust him and depend on him. She'd even told him about the infrequent but disturbing phone calls. He had notified the police immediately, had their phone number changed and answered the phone himself whenever he was in the house. There hadn't been another mystery call since.

She'd tried to tell Wade about her continued friendship with Glenn and Eloise and that she often visited them when she went into town, but the mention of Glenn's name enraged Wade, so she'd dropped the subject. Obviously Wade was having even more difficulty learning to trust than she was. Oh, there were times when she wondered if she was a fool to trust another man. She'd been suspicious the few times Wade had gone to Hooligan's with Britt. When Glenn had insinuated that her husband's taste in women ran to the baser types, she'd defended Wade, but the seed of doubt had been planted.

If only Wade loved her, she would trust him completely. But he didn't love her; he simply wanted her. And he wanted his son. She had never realized how difficult it would be to live with a man she knew didn't love her, when she loved him more and more each day. Watching her marriage to Tyler disintegrate had caused her a great deal of pain, but her love for Wade was far deeper and more passionate. If this marriage failed...

She'd thought about moving back into town, giving Wade and her some breathing space, letting him have a chance to decide if he wanted to spend the rest of his life in a second marriage without love. But the thought of being separated from him, even for a few days, didn't appeal to Lydia in the least. And she couldn't bear the thought of leaving Molly behind. Molly. That beautiful, tomboyish little girl who clung to Lydia, taking every ounce of mothering from her that she could give. Molly had been so hungry, so starved for genuine maternal affection.

And then there was Ruthie—that country-ignorant old woman with a heart as big as the universe and a wisdom as basic and honest as life itself. If she tried to leave the farm, Ruthie would probably hog-tie her to a fence.

Lydia picked up the cake and went outside. Molly and a dozen other girls and a few boys came running, circling the table where Lydia had placed the cake.

"Wow, Molly," a little freckled-faced redhead said, "that's the biggest cake I've ever seen. Did your new mama make it for you?"

"My mama bought it at the bakery in town," Molly announced with pride, grinning when the children oohed and aahed. "And she gave me this," the child pointed to the gold locket hanging on a gold chain around her neck. "She's going to give me jewelry every year for my birthday, forever and ever so that when I grow up I'll have as much pretty jewelry as she does." Molly picked up the Southern belle doll dressed in a wide-brimmed straw bonnet and hoop skirt. "And she gave me this doll so I can add it to our collection."

Lydia lit the candles, then gathered the children into a circle around the table. They sang "Happy Birthday," Molly blew out her candles and Tanya helped Lydia serve the refreshments while Molly opened her gifts.

"I've got to go," Tanya whispered to Lydia, then went over to where Ruthie sat in the swing under a big oak tree. "I'm going on home now," she told her mother-in-law, then rushed off before Ruthie could reply.

When Lydia sat down in the swing beside her, Ruthie nodded in the direction of Tanya's car. "She's mighty unhappy, that one. And all wrong for Britt, but he thinks he loves her."

"Do you think I'm all wrong for Wade?" Lydia asked the question partly out of genuine curiosity and partly to get Ruthie's mind off Tanya.

"I think you're the best thing that's ever happened to Wade. And to Molly, too."

"But I'm not a country girl. I'm a terrible cook. I hate chickens. And I'm a working wife, and I'm going to be a part-time working mother."

"Mmm...hmm. But you love my son, and you love his daughter, and one of these days when Wade realizes he loves you, we're going to be a mighty happy family."

"Do you think Wade loves me?" Lydia couldn't dare let herself hope. But if Ruthie thought...

"How's the party going?" Wade asked as he walked up behind his wife and mother.

Lydia jumped, then turned around and smiled at him, wondering how much of the conversation he'd overheard. "The party's winding down. Why don't you go over and check out your daughter's birthday bounty while I get you some cake and lemonade?"

"You sit right there and rest with Ma. I can get my own cake and lemonade."

Lydia thought her husband looked wonderful, despite the fact that his jeans were faded, his shirt dirty and torn, and he was wringing wet with perspiration. Watching him move made her think about the way he moved—next to her, over her, under her, on her—during the sweet hours of night, the hours when he really was her husband.

She watched him with his daughter. The way he looked at Molly, touched her, smiled at her. Lydia wondered if he'd love their child as much. Yes. She knew he would. Wade Cameron was a loving man.

If only he loved her.

Wade sat on the couch thumbing through the latest issue of the *Farm and Ranch Living* magazine. When an article entitled "Alabama Poultry Producing Second in the Nation" caught his eye, he skimmed it quickly but couldn't keep his mind focused on the subject. All he could think about was Lydia, about taking her to bed and making love to her. Ruthie and Molly had gone on up to bed about thirty minutes earlier, after Lydia's favorite Audie Murphy Western ended. It wasn't quite nine-thirty, and Lydia seemed totally engrossed in her cross-stitching.

He wanted to pull her up out of her chair, drag her over onto the couch beside him and hold her in his arms. But in the evenings when they shared a quiet hour or so with Ruthie and Molly, Lydia never sat on the couch with him. She had taken possession of the old wooden rocker that had belonged to his grandmother, and she sat there every night, working with her needle and thread. Often she watched television with Molly or talked to Ruthie about the garden or her ideas for the renovations she was determined to make in the farmhouse. But conversation between the two of them was strained, often forced. The only place they found a common ground was behind the closed doors of their bedroom. At night, lying in his arms, she was his wife. The rest of the time, she was Ruthie's favorite daughter-in-law, Molly's much-loved new mother, and his... friend?

Although his life with Lydia was a great improvement over his life with Macie, he didn't want things to stay the way they were. He wanted more. He wanted a real marriage.

Lydia had told him she loved him, but those words had been spoken in the throes of passion and never in the cold light of day. He couldn't be sure how she really felt about him. And he was plagued by doubts concerning his own feelings. Did he love Lydia? Was desiring a woman to the point of madness love? Was wanting her face to be the first you saw in the morning and the last at night love? Was thinking about a woman constantly, remembering the feel and smell and taste of her, love?

"I wanted to thank you for giving Molly a party." He laid the magazine on the coffee table and glanced over at his wife.

Her gentle gaze rested on him, and she smiled. "I loved it almost as much as Molly did. I always had birthday celebrations when I was growing up, and I want to make sure Molly has happy memories of her childhood."

"Ma always made us a cake or pie, but she didn't know anything about parties." Wade leaned over toward Lydia's chair. Inspecting the cloth she held, he noticed the design was of a little girl and a dog. "Is that for Molly's room?"

"I'm glad you're letting me redecorate her room." Lydia held the cross-stitch piece up for him to see. "She's so excited. We're using several different shades of pink. It's her favorite color, you know."

"I'm glad you didn't pay any attention to me when I told you not to put yourself out trying to be her mother." Wade didn't like to remember some of the cold and hateful things he'd said to Lydia. She had been kind and patient and understanding. Far more understanding than he'd had a right to expect. He had taken her away from a world of money and social position and given her a run-down farm, a depleted bank account and a husband who couldn't even tell her that he loved her.

"Ruthie and I have decided to do some work on the kitchen before I start on the nursery." Lydia watched his face for a reaction, knowing how opposed he'd been to her spending any of her own money doing repairs on his house.

"Lydia, about fixing things up… Well, I know you must hate living in a house like this, but—"

"I love this house. It has so much character."

Before he could comment, they both heard a truck drive up, then a door slam. Bear, Rawhide and Leo began barking, then quieted down. Suddenly the front door burst open. Britt stood in the hall, glaring into the living room. His hair was mussed, as if he'd been raking his fingers through it. There was a wild, angry look in his topaz eyes. He stomped in, stopping directly in front of Wade.

"Tanya's left me!" Britt slumped down on the couch beside his brother, letting his big hands fall between his knees.

"Have you been drinking?" Wade asked.

Lydia tensed, sucking in a deep breath as she laid her needlework aside. She'd been dreading this moment, wondering when it would happen and how Britt would react.

"I had one beer at Hooligan's. One damn beer. I'm as sober as a judge." Britt jerked a piece of paper from his jeans pocket. "She left me a note." He handed the letter to Wade.

"When did she leave?" Wade asked, glancing down at the piece of crumpled paper he held.

"We had another big fight, and I stormed out. It was just the same old crap. I didn't want to hear it. I thought I'd give her time to cool off, so I went to Hooligan's and sat around nursing a beer for three hours."

Wade read over Tanya's words quickly, then jumped off the couch, crushing the letter in his big hand. "She's leaving with Reverend Charles?"

"What?" Lydia gasped.

"Yeah." Britt ran his hands over his face, then slammed them together, entwining his fingers in a gesture both prayerful and angry. "She's leaving me and running off with the preacher."

Lydia trembled at the sight of Britt's scarred face. She had never seen such agony or such fierce rage. "Oh, my God." Lydia felt betrayed by her sister-in-law. Tanya had told her she was leaving Britt, that they couldn't make their marriage work, but she'd never mentioned another man.

"I've already been to town. They're gone, all right. His car was gone and his house was dark." Britt kicked over the coffee table, knocking a stack of magazines to the floor. "If I ever get my hands on them, I'll kill them both."

"You don't mean that," Wade said. "That's your anger talking. Believe me, I know. When I caught Macie in the barn with Donnie Finch, I wanted to kill them. But I didn't. They weren't worth it."

"Looks like the Cameron brothers are failures at picking their women. Macie wasn't anything but a first-class whore, and now Tanya, that sweet girl I've loved all my life, has run off with a preacher. A damned *preacher,* of all people." Britt's agonized laughter filled the farmhouse as he leaned over against the wall and began pounding his fists against the paneled surface.

"What's all the racket down here?" Ruthie, in her flowered cotton gown and housecoat, asked as she walked into the room. "Britt?"

"Tanya's left." Lydia stood up and went to Ruthie. "She's run off with Reverend Charles. She wrote Britt a note."

"Oh, Lord. I knew something like this was going to happen." Ruthie moved across the room toward Britt.

"Don't you say anything, Ma." Britt held up his hands as if to ward off his mother's approach.

"This ain't the end of the world, son. You and Tanya were wrong for each other from the beginning, just like Wade and Macie were. Time will take care of this, and you'll find the right woman."

"Just like my big brother has?" Britt cast Lydia a dark glance. "She may be pregnant, but if I were Wade I'd be questioning whether or not I was the father. My bet is that it's Haraway's kid. She can't seem to stay away from him.''

Lydia looked at Wade, saw the pain and distrust in his eyes. Not now, she prayed silently. Don't let him start doubting me again, not when we've finally made some progress in our relationship.

"What the hell is he talking about?" Wade asked her.

"I'm talking about the fact that every time she goes into town, she stops by to see Haraway. And sometimes she stays for hours." Britt glared at Lydia. "You can't tell him I'm lying, can you?"

"Shut your mouth, Britt Cameron!" Ruthie reached out and slapped her younger son's cheek. "Lydia visits Eloise Haraway. There ain't nothing between her and Glenn."

"If you believe that," Britt said, turning to his brother while he rubbed his smarting cheek, "then you're a bigger fool than I am."

"It's time you come with me." Ruthie grabbed Britt by the arm, jerked him to attention and maneuvered him out of the house and onto the porch.

Lydia turned to Wade. "I . . . I've tried to tell you several times that I stop by to visit Eloise and Glenn, but you . . . you—"

"I told you to stay away from Haraway." Wade reached out and grabbed her by the shoulders. "I thought I could trust you. I never thought you'd lie to me."

"I haven't lied to you." Tears formed in the corners of her eyes.

"You've been seeing Haraway behind my back."

"No, I haven't, I—"

Wade's big fingers bit into the soft flesh of her upper arms. "I'm not going to live with a woman I can't trust. You've come into my life and turned it upside down. You've made my daughter love you. You've gained my mother's respect, and all the while you've been lying and cheating—"

"Don't say any more," Lydia screamed, covering her ears with her hands. "You're upset about Britt and Tanya. You're remembering all those years with Macie. You're judging me by another woman's actions."

He released her, turned his back on her and knotted his hands into fists. "You're all alike. All of you. Sweet and soft and willing. You make a man crazy, make him want you, make him love you, and then you stick a knife in his gut."

"Please don't say these things. You don't mean them. You'll regret them tomorrow." Lydia opened her arms, reaching her hands out in a pleading gesture, a come-to-me signal.

"What I regret is marrying you, allowing you into my life, into my daughter's life. But you're pregnant and I'm stuck with you."

"No, you're not." Lydia dropped her hands to her sides. "I love you, Wade Cameron. I didn't want to love you, but I do. And I want our marriage to work, but I'm not going to stay here and take this kind of abuse."

When Lydia turned around and started out into the hallway, he called out, "Where do you think you're going?"

"I'm going upstairs to pack a bag, and then I'm going to drive into town. I'll stay at my house for a few days until you come to your senses. When you can tell me that you trust me, that you will do everything in your power to make our marriage work, then come into town and get me."

"If you think, for one minute, that I'll—"

"Oh, yes. I want one other thing. I want you to be able to tell me that you love me." Saying that, Lydia walked down the hallway and up the stairs.

Wade followed her into the hall, watching her until she disappeared into their room. He was staring into the emptiness when Ruthie came back into the house.

"While I was trying to cool Britt off, I could hear you and Lydia fighting." Ruthie shoved Wade toward the stairs. "Don't let her leave. Tell her what she wants to hear and tell her tonight."

"I'll be damned if I will."

"You'll be damned if you don't."

Wade gave his mother a killing stare, then turned around and walked out onto the porch where he found his brother sitting on the steps. He sat down beside him.

"Let's go to Hooligan's and get rip-roaring drunk," Wade said, putting his arm around his brother's shoulder.

Arm in arm the two men went over to Wade's truck, got in and drove off.

Twelve

Lydia paced the floor in her den, waiting for Ruthie Cameron. Her mother-in-law had called her twenty minutes ago and said she was getting one of the hired hands to drive her into town. Lydia didn't know what she was going to say to Ruthie.

She'd been gone from the farm two days, actually less than forty-eight hours. Ruthie had called twice yesterday; Molly had called five times. She'd tried to reassure her stepdaughter that her stay in town was only temporary, but when Molly had asked for an exact date when she'd be returning home, Lydia had been at a loss for words. Finally she had suggested that, since it was late June and Molly was out of school, her father might let her come into town and stay a few days. Molly had called back to say that Wade was thinking about it.

Lydia knew she'd taken a huge risk by moving out, by leaving the farm, by giving Wade an ultimatum. Her husband was a proud man. It would be difficult for him to come after her. Perhaps impossible.

But if he didn't love and trust her, then their marriage was truly doomed, and it was better to find it out now, before... before she fell even more in love with him... before she wouldn't be able to give up mothering Molly... before she couldn't bear to give up Ruthie's friendship and leave behind that wonderful old farm.

Eloise and Glenn had been inordinately pleased to see her return to town. Glenn had chosen his words carefully, being sure not to insult Wade when he'd told Lydia that he cared deeply for her and would honor whatever decisions she made concerning her future.

Lydia jumped when she heard the pecking sound at the glass doors. Quickly turning around, she saw Ruthie, smiling and waving. Lydia rushed to open the patio doors.

Ruthie gave Lydia a bear hug, then brushed fresh tears from her eyes. "I want you and me to take a little ride."

"I'm not going back to the farm until Wade comes and gets me."

"I want you to drive me over to Cotton Row. Wade's going to meet us there later." Ruthie looked around the den. "You can fix up the farmhouse to look as good as this place."

"Wade's going to meet us?"

"He don't know you're going to be there."

Lydia shook her head. "It won't work, Ruthie. You can't force him to love and trust me."

"Oh, hogwash. He loves you. He's just afraid to admit it. I've got a couple of stubborn boys."

"How's Britt?"

"He'll live. But I wish he'd stop spouting off about wanting to kill Tanya. Of course he'll shut up when the new wears off his pain."

"Have you heard from Tanya?"

"Nope, and I don't reckon I will. She's probably ashamed to talk to me, seeing how she ran off with the preacher. Always said he was too young and good looking to be a minister. And not married. That's asking for trouble." Ruthie took Lydia by the arm. "Get your purse and car keys, and let's go."

Arguing with Ruthie Cameron, Lydia had already discovered, was useless, so within ten minutes Lydia pulled her BMW into the overgrown drive in front of the old gin on Cotton Row.

Ruthie opened the door, stepping outside and moving her obese body slowly toward the gin. Stopping several yards away, she turned to Lydia.

"When I was a girl, this old gin was still running. My father's family built this gin and almost this whole side of the block."

Lydia took a good look at what remained of Cotton Row, which a hundred years ago had been the nucleus of Riverton, the hub of the community when cotton had still been king in the South. "I know you want to see these old buildings restored, but I doubt seriously that any development firm would be willing to cover the extra expense."

"Glenn Haraway has done everything he could to persuade me to sell, including threatening me." Ruthie glanced at her daughter-in-law.

"Threatened you? Glenn?"

"He's not the man you think he is. He's a lot like his father. Old Wallace Haraway was one crooked politician. He was a judge when he died. If you had enough money, you could get away with murder in Riverton twenty years ago."

"What are you trying to say?"

"I'm telling you not to trust Glenn Haraway. He's the kind of man who'll use whatever means necessary to get what he wants. He wants this property, and he wants you."

"I can't believe that—"

"I think Glenn was behind those mysterious phone calls you got. Whoever it was never did act on his threats, so it must have been somebody who didn't really want to hurt you, just wanted to scare you."

Lydia didn't want to believe Ruthie's accusations, but she had to admit that her reasoning made perfect sense. "Does Wade agree with you? Does he think Glenn is behind all those phone calls?"

"Yeah. That's one of the reasons he wanted you to stay away from Haraway."

Lydia breathed deeply, taking in the aroma of burning wood. "Ruthie, do you smell something burning?"

"My Lord, the gin's on fire. Look!"

Lydia looked out toward the old building. Billows of smoke streamed from the broken windows. Without warning, a small, wiry man ran out the side door of the gin and stopped dead still when he saw Ruthie and Lydia.

"Who's that?" Ruthie took several tentative steps in the man's direction.

"Ruthie wait. He could be an arsonist."

Suddenly the stranger pulled a gun from where he'd had it braced between his belt and his body. Approaching quickly, he shouted, "You two stay right where you are."

Lydia felt her heart racing, the blood pounding in her ears. When her mother-in-law started toward the gunman, Lydia grabbed her by the arm and pulled her backward.

"That's right. You make the old woman behave." He waved the gun around in the air. "Now, let's get going."

"Where are you taking us?" Ruthie demanded.

"Start marching toward the gin." He moved around behind them and stuck the gun in Lydia's back. "You don't do what I say and I'll shoot right now."

"Do as he says, Ruthie."

When they reached the burning building, the man opened the side door. "Get inside."

"You can't mean to put us in there," Lydia said. "If you force us inside, you'll be murdering us."

"You two done seen my face. I can't let you tell the police. I won't get the rest of my money from Mr. Har—" He gave Ruthie a push over the threshold. "Now, you." He put his hand on Lydia's back.

"Look, you may have been paid to set fire to this place, but you aren't a murderer, are you? Let us go, and I'll see that you have the best lawyer in the state. The person to blame is the man who hired you," Lydia said.

"I'm sorry, lady. I don't want to kill you or the old woman either, but my life won't be worth a damn if—"

"Glenn Haraway hasn't got the guts to kill anybody himself," Ruthie shouted from inside the gin, then coughed several times. "He hires people like you to do his dirty work."

"Shut up, will ya?" He gave Lydia a gentle nudge into the building, then slammed the door and locked it from the outside.

Ruthie, who was on her knees, reached up and pulled Lydia down. "The smoke's rising. If we get down low and crawl we've got a chance of getting around to the back door before we smother to death."

Lydia obeyed, both women getting down on all fours and moving slowly across the splintered wooden floor.

"Glenn hired that man to torch this place." Lydia couldn't bear to think about what a gullible fool she'd been, how she'd trusted Glenn, respected him, called him her friend.

"Now's not the time to be fretting about that. We've got to get out of here. Then we'll see to it that Haraway hangs from the highest tree in Tishomingo County."

Wade saw the smoke a block away and immediately knew that the old gin was on fire. He pulled his truck to a halt in the middle of the street in front of the building, jumped out and raced toward Lydia's car. Out of the corner of his eye, he saw a man locking the side door to the gin. The evening sunlight glinted off a metal object in the man's hand.

What the hell's going on? Wade wondered. Where was his mother? What was Lydia's car doing here, and where was she? Acting on gut-level instinct, Wade ran back to his truck, pulled down the shotgun hidden under the seat and turned on the man running from the gin. Without saying a word, Wade aimed the gun and fired. The shot landed at the arsonist's feet. He stopped dead still and stared at Wade.

"Where's my wife and my mother?" Wade asked, his voice deadly.

"I don't know what you're talking about." The man took several steps.

Wade aimed the gun and fired again, taking great satisfaction in seeing the stranger dance to the shotgun's tune. "I won't ask again."

"Dammit, man, I didn't want to do it. They knew I'd torched this place. The old woman even knew who'd hired me."

Wade aimed the shotgun again.

"I locked them in the building."

Wade ran over to the man, and holding the gun in his left hand, balled his right hand into a fist and slammed it hard into the man's face. He fell over backwards. Wade nudged him in the ribs with the tip of his boot to make sure he was unconscious. He was.

All Wade could think about was the two women he loved the most in the world. His wife and his mother. He dropped the gun to the ground. With trembling fingers, he fumbled with the locked door, and the minute it opened, he rushed inside. The smell of burning wood, the thick lung-clogging smoke, the heavy darkness hit him the moment he entered the smoldering gin. He dropped to the floor.

"Lydia! Ma!"

"It's Wade," Ruthie shouted.

When he heard his mother's voice, he thanked God. The heavy, dense smoke obliterated everything inside the gin from his view. "Where are y'all? I've got the door open. Can you come this way?"

Within seconds he saw his mother and Lydia crawl toward him. He reached down, grabbing Lydia up and into his arms.

"Get her out of here, boy. This smoke ain't done her or my grandson no good."

Running, Wade took Lydia outside, then turned to make sure his mother was safe. He smiled when he saw Ruthie emerge from the building, look around, pick up the shotgun and walk over to their unconscious attacker.

"You get Lydia to the hospital, fast," Ruthie said. "And send the police back here for me and this firebug."

Lydia held on to Wade as if letting go would end her life. She cried and coughed, then coughed and cried. "Oh, Wade, I was so scared. If anything's wrong with the baby because of this, I'll... I'll personally kill Glenn Haraway."

"You won't have to, honey. I'll do it for you." Wade ran his hand over Lydia's soot-covered face, knowing he'd never seen anything so beautiful in all his life. "God, woman, if anything had happened to you..."

"But it didn't. You saved us." Lydia reached out to touch his cheek and felt the dampness from his tears. "Wade?"

"I love you, Lydia. I love you." He kissed her, with all the hunger and passion and fear that raged inside him.

"Britt's going to take me and Molly on home, now," Ruthie said as she waved goodbye from the hospital room doorway. "We'll have everything ready for you two when you get home in the morning."

"Britt, you've got to keep things going on the farm. We're a family, and we've got to help each other. Ma and Molly and Lydia and I are depending on you." Wade sat on the bed beside his wife, one arm draped around her shoulder, the other resting beside hers, their hands entwined.

Molly ran over to Lydia, threw her arms around her and gave her a wet, sloppy kiss. "I love you, Lydia."

"I love you, too." Lydia squeezed Wade's hand.

"Come on. Let's get home so these two can be alone." Ruthie ushered her younger son and granddaughter out the door.

Wade leaned over, resting his forehead against his wife's. "Thank God, you and the baby are both all right."

"I don't see why I had to stay here overnight if—"

He put his finger on her lips to silence her. "Shh . . . The doctor said he wanted you to stay overnight just as a precaution, so we're going to stay overnight."

"You're going to get awfully uncomfortable sleeping on the floor."

"If you think I'm going to let you out of my arms for one minute tonight, you're crazy." Wade pulled her close, lowered his head and covered her mouth with his own.

The kiss was long and sweet and thorough. Wade raised his head. "I love you. I trust you, and I want to spend the rest of my life making you the happiest woman in the world."

"I'm sorry," she sighed, breathing deeply to keep from crying again. "I had no idea what kind of man Glenn Haraway was. Poor Eloise."

"I don't want to talk about Haraway. The police have him in custody, and you and Ma won't have to worry about testifying against him in court. Chief Landers told Britt that Haraway confessed to everything when his hired arsonist turned on him. Haraway thought that if all the old buildings were destroyed, he could persuade Ma to sell her property." Wade tightened his hold on Lydia, wanting to convey by his touch that he would always take care of her, that she would always be safe with him.

"Glenn must have been as ambitious as Tyler to go to such lengths to further his career."

"Seems this isn't the first time Haraway has used that man's services. Our firebug confessed that Haraway paid him to make phone calls harassing a certain woman I happen to love."

Lydia opened her mouth on a startled gasp, then closed it quickly, biting into her bottom lip as she tried to stem the flow of her tears. "I never once suspected Glenn."

"You didn't really know him."

"I hate to admit, but at one time I thought Britt might have been making the calls. He acts like he hates me."

"He doesn't hate you. He doesn't even really dislike you," Wade said, kissing her forehead. "Britt's just filled with a lot of anger and pain. Now that Tanya's gone, it's bound to get worse before it gets better."

"Well, it seems that you and I can't get out of the spotlight. No doubt we're the talk of the town again. You. Me. Glenn. The fire. Britt and Tanya and the preacher. Oh, Wade, aren't we ever going to have a normal, ordinary life? I just want to go home to the farm, be your wife and Molly's mother."

Wade massaged her neck with his fingertips, circling it with his big hand. "You don't know how much I want to make love to you, Mrs. Cameron. Two nights without you have been pure hell."

Lydia snuggled up against her husband, placing her hand on his stomach, then slowly sliding it downward until she covered the zipper of his jeans. "Have you ever made love in a hospital bed?"

Wade laughed loudly, covering her hand with his own. "You realize that if we get caught, it'll just give the busybodies something else to gossip about."

She unzipped his jeans, slipped her fingers inside and caressed him. "It'll be worth it." She leaned over, brushing her lips against his in a slow, seductive maneuver. "Besides, I've gotten used to our being the talk of the town."

Epilogue

Ten-year-old Molly Cameron, wearing a white and navy summer dress, served the punch while Ruthie, dressed in a blue linen suit, handed their guests the petit fours on china plates. Wade, attired in a tailor-made gray suit, grabbed three-year-old Hoyt Lee Cameron just as he was about to topple over a silk flower arrangement on the low table in front of the Chippendale sofa.

Lydia, sitting at her desk inside her office, watched through the open doorway. Six-week-old Ruth Ann nursed contentedly at her mother's breast.

Today was the grand opening of the new office for Interiors by Lydia in Riverton Mississippi's new pride and joy, the Cotton Row Mall. Lydia could hardly believe what a remarkable job the architects and contractors had done, combining old with new, in order to maintain the old-fashioned beauty and the priceless heritage that had once been the original Cotton Row. Several buildings had actually been saved, and others had been torn down and their contents used to construct the newer parts of the mall.

After Glenn Haraway had been found guilty on numerous counts and sent away to serve a lengthy prison term, the town council had approached Ruthie about selling her property, explaining that they had found new investors who were interested in saving a great deal of the original Cotton Row and incorporating it into the new mall. Ruthie had sold her heritage and invested the money in her family's future.

Wade set his son down inside the playpen in the corner of Lydia's office.

"I don't wanna stay in here," Lee whined.

"How do you think you'll get any work done, the days you plan to have the children down here? Lee has worn me out in the last thirty minutes." Wade watched his youngest child's little mouth as she sucked greedily on Lydia's breast. "She's almost as beautiful as her mother." He ran one finger over his daughter's cheek, then over onto his wife's full breast.

Lydia smiled up at him. "I'll only be down here half days until Ruth Ann is older. And don't worry about Lee. He's much better behaved when you're not around. Boys like to show off for their fathers."

"Mom, we're almost out of ginger ale," Molly said from the open doorway. "Is there any more back in the storeroom?"

"Molly's going to come here straight from school every day and baby-sit until quitting time," Lydia told her husband, then turned to Molly. "There's a whole other case back there."

"Wow, this grand opening is great. I've been showing potential clients pictures of our house, inside and out, before and after. Are they ever impressed." Molly ran toward the storeroom.

"You turned our old farmhouse into a showplace." Wade kissed his wife on the cheek.

"It's a good advertisement." Lydia looked down at her baby daughter who'd fallen asleep, her mouth open against her mother's breast. Easing the child away from her body, she handed her to Wade, then closed her nursing bra and buttoned the jacket of her yellow silk suit.

Wade laid his sleepy daughter down in the padded carryall atop Lydia's desk, tenderly tucking her soft white blanket around her. "I love you, Mrs. Cameron. You've made me a happy man." He put his arm around Lydia's waist and pulled her close to his side.

"I love you, and I want to show you just how much—tonight," she said before giving her husband a passionate, tongue-thrusting kiss.

"Will you two stop that," Molly teased. "What will people think? If you two keep doing things like that, y'all are going to be the talk of the town."

Wade and Lydia laughed, gazing into each other's eyes, exchanging a secret look that said, *Our life is good, isn't it, so who cares what anyone else thinks?*

*   *   *   *   *